Buried Treasures
of the Ozarks

Books in W. C. Jameson's *Buried Treasures* series:

Buried Treasures of the American Southwest
Buried Treasures of the Ozarks
Buried Treasures of Texas
Buried Treasures of the Appalachians
Buried Treasures of the South
Buried Treasures of the Rocky Mountain West
Buried Treasures of California
Buried Treasures of the Pacific Northwest
Buried Treasures of the Atlantic Coast
Buried Treasures of New England
Buried Treasures of the Great Plains

Buried Treasures
of the Ozarks

Legends of Lost Gold, Hidden Silver,
and Forgotten Caches

W.C. Jameson

August House / *Little Rock*
P U B L I S H E R S

Published 1990 by August House, Inc.,
P.O. Box 3223, Little Rock, Arkansas 72203,
501-372-5450.

Printed in the United States of America

10 9 8 7 6 5 4 3

LIBRARY OF CONGRESS CATALOGING-IN-PUBLICATION DATA
Buried treasures of the Ozarks :
legends of lost gold, hidden silver, and forgotten caches /
W.C. Jameson—1st edition.
p.   cm.
Includes bibliographic references.
ISBN 0-87483-106-7
1. Treasure-trove—Ozark Mountains Region.
2. Legends—Ozarks Mountains Region.
3. Ozark Mountains Region—Miscellanea.
I.Title.
F417.09J35   1990
976.7'1—dc20   89-77327

Cover illustration by Wendell E. Hall
Typography by Heritage Publishing Co.
Design direction by Ted Parkhurst
Project direction by Hope Norman Coulter
Editorial assistance by Ed Gray

This book is printed on archival-quality paper that meets the
guidelines for performance and durability of the Committee on
Production Guidelines for Book Longevity of the
Council on Library Resources.

AUGUST HOUSE, INC.   PUBLISHERS   LITTLE ROCK

For my mother

Contents

Prologue

Not all of the tales included in this book were easily ac-
quired. Some could be had merely for the asking; others were
available from writings and literature of the area. Many of them
had to be tracked down.

Some of the tracking and hunting of these tales occurred in
various libraries throughout the Ozarks. Searching the dark
stacks of the musty libraries is, in some ways, like pursuing a
quarry in the wild Ozark mountains and forests: The quarry
sometimes blends in with the surroundings and is not easily
located, but the determined tracker persists and is eventually
rewarded.

Many of these tales had to be tracked in the Ozark Mountains
themselves, doggedly followed and occasionally cornered. A
few of them got away, but many were captured. Tracking the
stories in the wild meant traveling to remote parts of Arkansas,
Missouri, and Oklahoma, visiting and getting to know many of
the deep Ozark denizens up close and personally. In the course
of this effort I have put thousands of miles on my vehicle and
discovered some of the most inaccessible roads imaginable. I
have leaned across many a split-rail fence talking to an Ozark
old-timer who might be able to shed light on some long-obscure
aspect of a particular story.

I have stared across campfires into the eyes of men who have
searched for these lost treasures, listening closely as they spoke
of their experiences and of their knowledge of locations, circumstances, and insights into the minds of those who buried riches
lifetimes ago.

I have sat in awe in rustic log cabins while old men, in the finest Ozark storytelling tradition, related some of these tales, filling them and the listener with the wonder and magic of the unknown, of mysteries long unsolved.

I have met and visited men who have committed nearly their entire lives to the search for the wealth they believe lies just beyond the next bend or deep within the next cave.

Given a choice between prowling the libraries and stalking these tales in the wild, I prefer the latter, mainly because in so doing, one gets the stories directly from the Ozark folk themselves, from the lips of those who know the mountains and the woods, the animals and the weather, the rivers and the rocks.

In listening to these stories firsthand one receives not only the tale, but the spirit of the tale as well. That spirit is in many ways related to the spirit of the folk—a never-say-die attitude that has enabled the mountain people to survive in the remote corners of rugged and often forbidding Ozark environments. In addition to the tales, it is this spirit we wish to capture and preserve between the pages of this book.

In nearly every case where I gleaned some element of a tale from an Ozark native, I perceived in the people what I can only describe as a restless passion for the story—not just for the wealth they surely hoped to locate, but for the story itself. Many of the Ozarkers with whom I visited not only believe every word of these tales, they believe *in* the stories themselves as if the stories were icons of their Ozark existence. They believe the stories belong to them, are their property. For the most part the stories are not to be shared with a neighbor or an outsider. Handed down from generation to generation, they are the real treasures, and they are often closely guarded.

Because of that perception, many of those I visited with refused to reveal anything and would sometimes chase me away. Others, a bit more relaxed, were still suspicious and guarded, as if they thought I wanted to steal from them not only the treasures but their tales of the treasures. Very few were casual in releasing information. Some were a little more willing to disclose a few facts; others only dangled vague references before my imagination.

Many Ozarkers still search for these treasures. Some, according to their claims, actually find one. Most do not.

Even when they are frustrated at not finding wealth—no doubt much as their fathers and grandfathers were frustrated—they all retain a passion for the search and the story, a passion that is surely inherited from their elders.

Most of those I encountered were of a single type, loners and outcasts, without families and operating on the fringes of society. All were dreamers, dreaming not only of treasure but of the adventure of the search. Their dreams are what sustain them, drive them on.

All of them were men.

In getting to know them, I sometimes felt as if I were looking at the mountains themselves. The men were lined, wrinkled, and weathered like the layers of weathered limestone that make up the foundations of these hills. Many of them were bent like aged trees still clinging to precarious slopes, extending their roots deeper and deeper into the crevices in the never-ending search for water and sustenance.

Indeed, these men are a product of the land, offspring of the loins of the hills and hollows. To read these tales is to take a journey into the deep Ozarks, a journey that begins and ends with the people.

W.C. Jameson

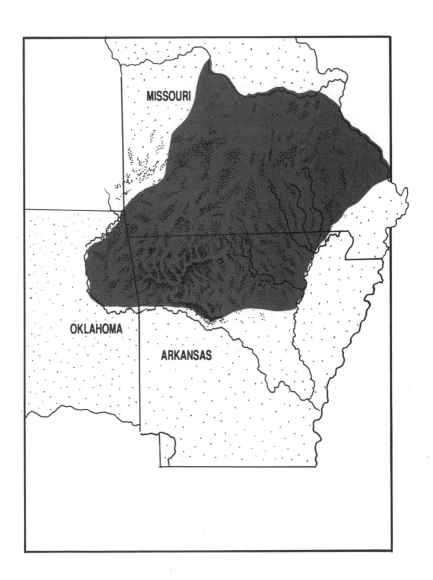

Introduction

In history, folklore, culture, and geography, the Ozark Mountains have been described as "remote," "secluded," "dark," "forbidding," "lawless," "dangerous," and "mysterious." These terms might seem inflated, but many of them are still applied today to this unique range of hills and valleys. In spite of their location near major cities, the Ozark Mountains remain in many ways dark, unexplored, and mysterious.

These grand mountains comprise significant portions of northwestern Arkansas, southern Missouri, and northeastern Oklahoma. A tiny part of the Ozarks even extends into the extreme southeastern corner of Kansas. Consisting of approximately 60,000 square miles of uplifted and dissected plateau, the Ozarks are bounded on the north by the Missouri River, on the east by the Mississippi River, on the southeast by the Black River, and on the south by the Arkansas River. The western boundary of the Ozark Mountains is less distinct, but geologists define it as where the 325-million-year-old rock gives way to younger Pennsylvanian Age rock, not so much a boundary as it is a gradual transition. Generally speaking, most investigators refer to the Neosho River in Oklahoma as the western boundary.

ORIGINS

The Ozarks had their origin in darkness, the darkness associated with the great depths of a long-ago sea. For hundreds of millions of years, the portion of the North American crust that was to become the Ozark Mountains was subjected to periodic uplift and sinking as a result of various violent forces taking place within the earth.

Approximately 280 million years ago, after the most violent of the land-forming episodes had ceased, the region that was to become the Ozarks was a flat featureless plain perched high above the seawaters that covered much of the North American continent at the time. This plain was subjected to constant erosion from rain and runoff for the next 180 million years, a process that eventually eroded the plain nearly to sea level.

There followed an episode of rising seawaters that effectively covered this low flat plain, submerging it again to great depths for the next 65 million years. During this period, more sediments accumulated upon the submerged structure, layer upon layer, and eventually hardened to form thick strata of limestone and sandstone.

About 30 million years ago the area was subjected to uplifting, and once again another flat plain was elevated several thousand feet above sea level.

The climate began to change dramatically around this time: Temperatures gradually dropped and rains fell incessantly. As the temperature cooled over the centuries, the rains turned to snow, which accumulated at the higher elevations, eventually becoming compressed, turning into ice, and forming glaciers.

After several thousand more years passed, the climate changed and the area gradually became warmer. The vast accumulations of snow and ice began to melt, and the meltwater began a headlong rush to the sea. This rapidly flowing, sediment-laden water began to carve into the soft limestone layers, removing material at a great rate and initiating the carving and sculpting of the limestone rock into many deep, narrow, steep-walled valleys that were soon to characterize this mountain range.

While the sculpting of the Ozark landscape was taking place on the surface, a different kind of sculpting was going on underground. The highly soluble limestone rock that makes up most of the Ozark range was being eaten away by the chemically active ground waters, forming vast cavern systems.

The climate entered yet another warming period and eventually stabilized about 4,000 years ago. During this time seeds of oak, hickory, and pine became established on the dissected landscapes of the Ozark uplift. Forests soon grew and prospered, and the environment took on an appearance that has remained essentially unchanged to the present. Thus the Ozark Mountains stood in relative isolation for several thousand years. The dense woods and valleys filled with many different types of wildlife. To an observer, it would have been hard to believe that processes of violent upheaval and dramatic weathering produced such a serene sylvan landscape. But serene it was, almost paradise-like. Paradoxically, while much of the rest of the North American continent was being occupied by descendants of Asians who crossed the land bridge between Alaska and Russia, the seemingly inviting recesses of the Ozark Mountains saw very little human occupation until relatively recent historical times.

EXPLORATION AND SETTLEMENT

What little we know of the Paleo-Indian populations of the Ozarks comes from the few sophisticated archaeological studies that have been conducted. Evidence suggests that the Ozarks were visited from time to time by groups of Native Americans but never significantly populated by them in historic times. Why the lush valleys of the Ozarks did not lure great numbers of Indians remains a mystery. Some have suggested that the tribes that settled on the fringes of the Ozarks held the distant dark range in awe, even fear. Many early Indians believed the Ozarks were populated by demons.

During the historic period, Osage, Illinois, Caddo, and Quapaw tribes began to move into and occupy isolated locales in the interior of the range, but their numbers were always small. The Caddo and Osage people briefly established small settlements but were subsequently removed to reservations in Indian Territory.

Spanish explorers visited the Ozarks around 1555 in search of precious metals. Evidence of Spanish occupation and mining in the area is plentiful, but their time in the region was short and they established no permanent settlements. Reports and tales of gold and silver taken by the Spanish from the Ozark Mountains are legion.

By the beginning of the eighteenth century the French had entered the Ozarks and were the first whites to establish permanent settlements in the region. By 1702, they were mining lead from Ozark rock.

The French were also instrumental in establishing trading posts along the eastern margins of the Ozarks. From these locations they often penetrated the range and entered into trade with the small Indian populations there. The French, aware of the potential of a growing fur trade, also engaged in trapping the rich beaver streams in the deep valleys.

Silver was discovered once again in the Ozarks, this time by the French, and by 1725 several mining communities had become established. The discovery of silver provided the incentive to conduct sophisticated exploration of the interior for more of this ore as well as for gold.

News of the discoveries of silver, along with the lure of rich trapping grounds, stimulated the movement of whites into the region. By 1803, this migration increased even more rapidly because of the Louisiana Purchase.

In 1818 small numbers of Cherokee Indians from southern states such as South Carolina and Georgia began migrating into the Ozarks and establishing several large farms and successful homesteads. The Cherokee intermarried with members of the other tribes already inhabiting the region. There was also some intermarriage with early white settlers as well as with slaves who had escaped and sought refuge in the remote range.

In the 1820s, the Ozarks were becoming a refuge for still other Indian tribes that were gradually being displaced from their homelands by white settlers pushing westward. Among these recent immigrants were Peorias, Miamis, Kickapoos, and Creeks, some 6,000 Indians altogether.

In 1838, the United States government initiated a mass displacement of the Five Civilized Tribes of Southern Indians (Cherokee, Chickasaw, Choctaw, Creek, and Seminole) into Indian Territory (now Oklahoma), a movement that was linked to the Trail of Tears and that continued throughout the early 1840s. Hundreds of Indians passed through or near the Ozarks during this migration and, when they had the opportunity, escaped into the rugged wilderness knowing they would not be pursued by the military escort.

By this time there existed a curious mix of cultures living in the Ozark Mountains: the earlier Cherokee arrivals, who had initiated flourishing farming ventures; remnant French settlers; recent arrivals of displaced Indians from Kansas and Missouri; and escapees from the Trail of Tears. These different people were competing for limited farming lands. Their cultural diversity exacerbated tensions, and the situation became volatile. Fighting and killing occurred with frightening frequency. Violence was the order of the day.

Soon more and more whites were moving into the region. Settlement was slow owing to the difficulty of travel, the remoteness, the narrow valleys, and the thin soils, but still they came, slowly but consistently, and the more that arrived, the greater the potential for competition and violence.

Many of the white newcomers resented the ownership of vast tracts of land by Indians. Having difficulty displacing the Indians by vigilante means, the whites convinced the U.S. government to remove the Cherokees to Indian Territory. As soon as this was accomplished, the whites moved in and took over the old Cherokee holdings.

Many of the Indians, however, remained in hiding in the Ozarks. Angered at the acquisition of their property by greedy whites, they reacted violently. The Indians were legally declared outlaws and were pursued by armed posses. Indian gangs continued to roam the Ozarks inflicting vengeance on white settlers.

To add to the Indians' problems, white settlers continued to migrate into the area in ever greater numbers. During the

17

decade before the Civil War, the Ozarks experienced an influx of settlers from Kentucky, Tennessee, North Carolina, Virginia, and Pennsylvania. These newcomers were primarily of Scots-Irish descent and have been described as a restless, uneducated, adventurous frontier type. Most of them were searching for free land on which to homestead and raise their crops and families.

A wealthier group, mainly slave-owners from some of the same districts of the South, moved into and settled the better river bottoms where the slaves could be used to clear timber and plant tobacco, hemp, and corn. They were followed by capitalists attempting to take advantage of a perceived prosperity in the Ozarks. This latter group eventually became community leaders and initiators of change.

Still others arriving in the Ozarks were the so-called "poor white trash" who were run out of many of the eastern and southern states. This group included a criminal element that preferred to prey on the established settlers rather than work for themselves.

The new white arrivals added even more ingredients to an already tense and fragile mix of residents; conflict and violence became even more common.

The Civil War saw renewed interest in the settlement of the Ozarks. Some railroad construction was started as well as some timbering, commercial agriculture, and prospecting. Many of the immigrants arriving during this time were from the northern states and had badly needed capital for financing many of these endeavors.

Following the Civil War, the Ozarks became a refuge for a variety of lawless refugees from both North and South. Many of these men had nothing to return to. Their homes and villages had been burned, looted, and destroyed during the war. Many of them turned outlaw and gradually drifted toward the Ozarks, for it was generally known that the mountains were without law. The Ozarks took on a fearful reputation as the realm of predatory gangs of bandits, hostile Indians, and renegade ex-soldiers—a place for honest settlers to avoid.

Disorder and struggle in the Ozarks during this time was

becoming a way of life. Horse and cattle theft and even murder were common. The Ozark Mountains became synonymous with violence and death. Travelers gave the range a wide berth. Many honest God-fearing farmers, frightened of the growing lawlessness, moved from the isolated interior of the mountains—where hills and hollows offered the greatest sanctuary to outlaws—to more protected settlements near military outposts. The mountaineers who remained were clannish, isolated, and wild.

A third phase of settlement began with World War II, and the population grew steadily—though always slowly—from then on. The region continued to be perceived as a barrier as a result of poor or nonexistent roads, impassable valleys and rivers, limited agricultural potential, and isolation. Though more populated, the mountains were home to people who were as clannish and violent as ever. It has been said that the rugged and hostile land of the Ozark Mountains has shaped the people, and, until recently, the people have not had much success in shaping the land. Elements of a twentieth-century frontier culture can still be found along the few back roads that penetrate the remote hollows of the dark Ozark range.

Despite improvements in modern transportation, much of the Ozarks remains tucked away far from the mainstream of contemporary civilization. As the twenty-first century draws near, more and more of the younger Ozark natives are lured by the urban areas. Once they have begun careers and enjoyed the cultural diversions of the cities, they are loath to return to the hollows. Thus, in parts of the Ozarks the population is decreasing and many old homesteads are being abandoned in the isolated wilderness.

WEALTH IN THE OZARKS

The potential for discovering gold and silver in the Ozarks has fascinated people for centuries. De Soto's soldiers, on a mission from the Spanish royalty, explored and prospected the region in search of precious ores, carrying away enough to fill a treasury. The silver mines of the French and those of other later arrivals flourished for a time and then faded.

But there is wealth of another kind to be found in the Ozark Mountains—the wealth of a wonderfully rich folk tradition that includes music, dance, food, language, architecture, and tales. Interwoven through this rich tapestry of folk culture and history are many exciting tales about the search for lost mines and buried treasure. The Ozark Mountains inspire such stories. The history, the culture, and the geography all combine to generate an environment of wonder, magic, and tradition that give rise to awesome narratives of the place and the time.

The lure of buried treasure is powerful; hundreds have succumbed to it over past generations. Tales of lost and buried treasure in the Ozarks descend from the days of Spanish explorers, French traders and miners, Indians, and outlaws. Many who inhabit the Ozark Mountains today are descended from these very people.

While many of the farms and homesteads in the Ozarks did not flourish, the stories did. Some of the poor possessionless few who survived the rugged environment searched for, and occasionally found, hidden treasures in the remote hills and valleys of the range. Most of them aspired to wealth that eluded them. Most were unlucky, some fared better, many died trying.

People come and go, but the tales live on. The stories tell of lost and buried fortunes and of the ancient mines; they tell of ingots of pure silver and gold; they tell of the eternal quest for that which lies just out of sight beyond the next bend or just under a few feet of earth.

ARKANSAS

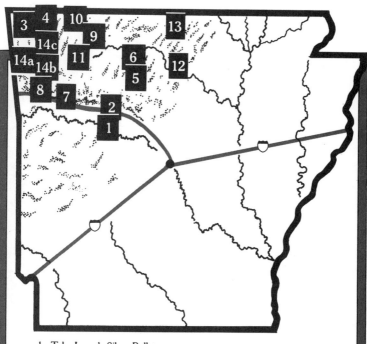

1. Tobe Inmon's Silver Bullets
2. The Mystery of the Turtle Rock
3. The Cave of Spanish Gold
4. The Madre Vena Ore Cache
5. Spanish Silver in Searcy County
6. The Lost Tabor Mine
7. Lost Aztec Mine in Franklin County
8. The Lost Tunnel of Gold
9. King's River Silver
10. The Buried Treasure of Mill Ford Cave
11. Lost Silver Mine near Huntsville
12. Stone County Silver
13. Old Man Napier's Hidden Treasure
14. Civil War Treasures
    a. The Lost Payroll
    b. Buried Arms at Cross Hollow
    c. Hidden Treasure on Callahan Mountain

Tobe Inmon's Silver Bullets

During the last two decades of the nineteenth century, there was significant westward migration from Kentucky, Tennessee, Virginia, and Alabama. Many of the migrants made it as far west as the rich agricultural and mining fields of California, but some got no farther than the Arkansas Ozarks, where they were lured by the promise of decent land.

All had reasons for leaving their homes in the East—a sense of adventure, the potential wealth awaiting them in the California gold fields, or simply desire for a better way of life. Some migrants had been chased out of their home area for one reason or another; they too found their way to and settled in the Ozark Mountains. Shunned, even persecuted, by cliquish neighbors and referred to as "poor white trash," most of those who abandoned the Appalachian valleys were humble, uneducated, and used to scraping out a meager living from the land and subsisting on very little.

Tobe Inmon was a resident of one poor valley in western Kentucky who managed to eke out a precarious existence for himself and his family by growing some corn on a rocky hillside and raising hogs and chickens in the bottoms. Inmon and his family did not get along well with their neighbors, and he earned a reputation as a recluse, neither needing nor wanting the company of others.

When Inmon was accused of stealing a neighbor's livestock and threatened with his life, he packed his few possessions, loaded his wife and two young boys onto a wagon, and left Kentucky. They headed west, driving their few hogs ahead of them as they traveled. They had no idea of their destination as they followed a long and arduous journey over country that offered little but mud, swamps, and misery.

One day Inmon somehow got off the main trail, got lost, and in searching for a way through the mountains found a little valley that immediately appealed to him. It was rather narrow with a running stream in the bottom and plenty of floodplain for a crop of corn. There appeared to be forage for his hogs and abundant timber for a cabin, some pens, and firewood. Another element of the valley that was attractive to Inmon was that the nearest neighbors lived over two miles away.

Deciding that setting up residence here was more appealing than continuing the tiring journey, Inmon went about the task of constructing a one-room log cabin and some pens for his livestock. When he had time he planted some corn at the flat area near the creek. Life was beginning to look good.

The nearest settlement of any importance was Dover, a small town some twelve miles south of Inmon's Moccasin Creek Valley farm, an important stop along the old road to Fort Smith. Occasionally Inmon would haul some chickens or a hog into Dover and trade for staples like flour, sugar, and coffee. The residents of Dover considered him a curious figure. He rarely spoke except to conduct what little business he had, and even then he was quite surly, preferring to conclude his affairs and leave town as soon as possible.

Inmon dressed in little more than rags and always appeared unclean. The few times he brought his family into town, they too looked wretched and ragged. Those who chanced by Inmon's homestead in the valley remarked at the squalor in which the family lived, claiming the log cabin had large open chinks that let in the cold air and appeared to offer only a little more shelter than the hog pen.

One day during the autumn of 1903, Inmon rode into Dover and asked for a doctor. His youngest son had come down with fever and was unconscious. Inmon was directed to Dr. Benjamin

Martin, the only doctor in town, who agreed to follow him out to Moccasin Creek. Martin was an affable man in his late forties, was well-liked by the community, and had delivered virtually every child in the town and the surrounding area under ten years old. The doctor was appalled at the primitive conditions in which the Inmon family lived, but he agreed to remain at the youth's bedside until he was out of danger.

Finally the fever passed and Martin prepared his horse and carriage for the return trip to Dover. As he was hitching the animal to the trace, Inmon appeared from around one corner of the cabin and asked the doctor about his fee. Aware of the man's poverty, Martin told Inmon he could just settle up when times got better and not to worry about it until then. Inmon was insistent, however, and finally offered the doctor a small canvas sack containing about thirty bullets for a large-caliber rifle.

During this time bullets were scarce. Most people who had need of them were happy to get them when they could. Martin examined the bullets and found them to be well-made, and as he was an enthusiastic hunter and sportsman, he accepted them gratefully as payment.

As the doctor packed the little sack of shells away in the carriage, he asked the farmer where he had gotten such fine ammunition. Inmon explained that he had made the bullets himself with lead he extracted from "an old mine back in the hills not too far from the cabin." Martin thanked him again, climbed onto his carriage, and returned to Dover.

At home Martin placed the sack of bullets on a shelf in his study, intending to use them on his next deer hunt. Over the next few weeks, however, he stayed busy treating the sick and delivering babies, and as a result his autumn deer hunt had to be postponed. He gradually forgot about the sack of shells lying on the shelf of his bookcase.

A full two years passed before the doctor remembered the bullets. While readying his equipment for a deer hunt, he located the sack of bullets on the shelf and placed them on the desk in his study so he would not forget to take them along the next morning. That evening, while reading at his desk, he picked up one of the bullets and turned it over and over in his fingers. Presently he scratched the tip of the bullet, trying to pick off some of the black residue. As some of the surface coating was removed, he noticed a peculiar color beneath.

On a hunch the doctor canceled his deer hunt. The next day he went to Russellville, a larger settlement a few miles south of Dover, and took the bullets to a friend knowledgeable about minerals. He discovered, to his astonishment, that they were made of pure silver. Martin sold the sack of shells for seventy-two dollars.

On returning to Dover that evening, Martin made plans to depart for the Inmon homestead the first thing in the morning to try to convince the poor farmer to show him the location of his so-called lead mine.

At sunrise the next day, Martin flogged his poor horse the entire trip to Moccasin Creek Valley. His carriage bounced along the seldom-used road until it seemed it would fall apart.

When the doctor arrived at the Inmon home he found it deserted; the site had apparently been unoccupied for several months. He drove the carriage to the farm of the nearest neighbor, asked the Inmons' whereabouts, and was told they had packed up and departed for Texas six months earlier. No one knew exactly where in Texas they had gone.

With what little light there was left in the day, Martin climbed the low hill just behind the Inmon cabin and wandered through the woods, inspecting every rock outcrop he encountered for any evidence of mining. He searched until darkness prevented him from continuing and he finally had to return to Dover.

The next morning found Martin busily outfitting himself with camping gear and provisions for an extended stay out at Moccasin Creek Valley. On this trip, he stayed for two and a half weeks, living in the deserted ramshackle cabin and exploring the hills and woods in search of the lost silver mine. After exhausting his food supply, he was forced to return to town.

Immediately on arriving home, Martin busied himself with preparations for an even longer stay at the valley in search of the ore. As he bustled around town, people remarked on his unshaven and filthy appearance and thought he acted strangely. He refused to tell people what he was doing and ignored pleas for his medical services. He was consumed with finding the fortune in silver he firmly believed existed in some hidden shaft in the Ozark Mountains near the old Inmon farmstead.

Over the next two years Martin continued to make forays into the hills behind the old Inmon cabin in search of the mine. Each time he was disappointed. Back in Dover, his patients gave up on him and sought another doctor to treat them.

Eventually Martin ran out of money and had to sell his home and practice in order to finance his search for the elusive silver. Finding the mine had become his all-consuming passion. Many residents of Dover were convinced the man had gone insane.

More years passed, and the long and unsuccessful search for Tobe Inmon's silver mine left Martin broke, broken, and disheartened. He finally moved in with a sister living in Russellville. His health began to deteriorate rapidly, and he died of complications from pneumonia.

On learning the story of Tobe Inmon's silver bullets, several Dover residents took up the search. During the years after Martin's death, many treasure hunters combed the hills and valleys around Moccasin Creek Valley. Some of them discovered ancient tools that were later identified as being of Spanish origin, thus giving rise to the belief that the early Spanish explorers in Arkansas under the leadership of De Soto had mined the region. Aside from the tools nothing else was found.

Could it be that Tobe Inmon had stumbled onto a long-lost Spanish silver mine? It is likely that this was the case. Poor Tobe. With all his poverty, he apparently had his hands on a fortune in silver, but he did not recognize it for what it was. And poor Dr. Martin: he recognized what it was but could never locate the source of the wealth.

In the summer of 1951, a Cherokee Indian named Lawrence Mankiller brought a large nugget into Fort Smith, where it was identified as a piece of high-grade silver. Mankiller stated that he had found the nugget on the floor of an old mine shaft while deer hunting in Moccasin Creek Valley. He had sought shelter from a rain shower in the convenient shaft, and while sitting just inside the entrance, he poked around in the rubble on the floor of the shaft and found the nugget.

Mankiller received an offer of several hundred dollars from a group of men who wanted him to lead them to the old shaft. Mankiller agreed to the proposition, pocketed the money, and promised to take them to the shaft the next morning. That night, however, Lawrence Mankiller disappeared and was never seen again.

Piney Page, the late Ozark folklorist, was raised in and around the Moccasin Creek Valley. He told the story of a relative who, while plowing a corn field on the floodplain where Moccasin Creek joins Shop Creek, paused in his labors to take a drink from the cool stream. While young Grover Page was lying on his stomach sipping creek water, he spied an object on the bottom that looked different from the rest of the stream gravel. On retrieving it, he discovered it was a silver nugget the size of a man's big toe.

The Page family had the nugget assayed and, on the encouragement of the evaluation, began to explore the creek area for the source of the ore. Some distance up the narrow valley through which runs Shop Creek, a thin seam of silver mixed with lead was discovered on a west-facing outcrop. The Pages invested in some mining equipment and blasted and drilled the weathered limestone rock in pursuit of the vein of ore. Considerable effort was expended and initially a large amount of silver was extracted, Page recalled, but the seam was soon lost. The Pages continued to work the small mine intermittently over the next six years, but the return was discouraging and ultimately they turned their attention back to farming.

A man who lives near Moccasin Creek Valley claims that on dark overcast nights associated with the waning moon, strange lights appear on the ridges adjacent to the valley, "dancing along the ridge crests." Mexicans and Indians have long believed that mysterious lights such as these appear above pockets of gold and silver. They explain that the lights represent spirits of the dead whose mission is to guard the ore and protect it from those who are not worthy, for anyone who removes the ore for selfish profit will be cursed. If one believes in such folklore, then the presence of the dancing lights in Moccasin Creek Valley may indicate that the silver is still there, still protected by the spirits, as elusive as it was to Benjamin Martin over seventy-five years earlier.

Perhaps someday the spirits will decide to relinquish their hold on the silver treasure that lies in these hills and smile upon the searcher who stumbles onto Tobe Inmon's lost mine.

The Mystery of the Turtle Rock

Piney Page was the source of another tale of buried trea-sure in Pope County. Growing up in the rural part of the county, he heard many stories about lost and buried Spanish gold and silver in the area of Piney Creek between Pilot Rock Mountain and Ford Mountain, but the one that fascinated him most was the one an uncle told him concerning the mysterious turtle rock.

Around 1910, as Page recalled it, an old-timer named Mose Freeman went out to gather his corn crop from the bottoms adjacent to Big Piney Creek where it makes a horseshoe bend between the two mountains. When he arrived, he noticed two men camped in the wooded area next to his field. Freeman intended to go talk to the two men after he picked his corn, to see if they carried any news from the bigger settlements in the southern part of the county. Visitors were scarce in this valley and Freeman always looked forward to having company.

But the two men seemed to be trying to stay out of his sight. One of them was a short mean-looking half-breed with a scar that traversed the entire length of his face, and the other was tall and gangly and appeared to take orders from the short man.

Presently the two men came out of the woods and furtively approached Freeman, saying they wanted to ask him some questions. They wanted to know if he was aware of any old carvings of snakes or turtles on the exposed rock in the area.

Freeman thought this was a strange question but he allowed as how he had never seen anything like this. On hearing his

30

reply, the two men showed no interest in continuing the conversation and promptly returned to their camp in the woods. Freeman went back to picking corn. He decided that he did not like the looks or manner of the pair and would have little or nothing to do with them. One morning a few days later, the two strangers were observed leaving the vicinity, riding a wagon that was piled high with camping gear and pulled by two sickly-looking horses. They appeared to be in a hurry to leave and acted nervous if anyone approached them. Both men carried rifles and displayed them aggressively when anyone ventured too close to the wagon.

The day following their departure, Mose Freeman and one of his sons went down to the deserted camp in the woods to look around. The camp was a poor one and they saw nothing of significance. Out in the woods a short distance from the camp, however, Freeman discovered several holes that had been dug around a large beech tree. On the tree was an old and weathered figure of a snake carved into the trunk. The snake was about three feet long, curving up the trunk of the tree, and its head was pointed downward. History records that the Spaniards used images of snakes and turtles to indicate the locations of buried treasure. The reptile's head was supposed to point toward the hidden wealth.

About twenty paces north of the old beech tree, Freeman found a large rock that appeared to have been recently dug up, turned over, and then set back down in its original location. With the help of his son and some poles they used as levers, he turned the rock back over. There, on the newly exposed side of the large limestone slab, was the carved image of a turtle. The rock had been laid over a freshly excavated hole about two feet deep, and in one corner of the excavation Freeman found a pot-sized hole from which a container had evidently been removed. Whatever the two strangers had unearthed during their search will probably never be known, because they were never seen again.

Stories of carved images of turtles on the limestone rock in Pope County are common. Several natives of the area have seen them, and a few have associated them with tales and legends of buried Spanish treasure. Most believe they are just that, tales and legends, having nothing to do with buried gold or silver. But historians point out that everywhere the Spanish have engaged in mining, both in North and South America, such carvings are quite common.

In 1976, a geology professor associated with a small college in Missouri was conducting a field studies class through the foothills of the Ozark Mountains. The professor and his students spent several days in Pope County examining the unique stratigraphy and collecting fossils from the Ozark limestone. The students were required to record their discoveries in a field journal and to keep a photographic record of their observations and collections. After eight days in the field, one of which was in the Big Piney Creek area, the professor and his students returned to Missouri.

One afternoon several days later, the professor, seated in his office, was going over the journals and photographs turned in by the students. One photograph in particular attracted his attention. It was a picture of a large flat piece of limestone rock, on the top of which could be seen the dim outline of a turtle. The only visible landmark in the photograph was an oak tree that looked very old.

The professor, who had heard legends of buried treasure in Pope County and of its association with carved images, became quite excited about the photograph. When he contacted the student who had taken it, however, she was unable to remember the location of the rock.

The professor has returned to the same area with other classes several times, but so far he has been unable to locate the turtle rock. Could it have been the same one found by Mose Freeman? Or could it be a different one, one that points to the existence of some long-hidden Spanish treasure? The search continues.

The Cave of Spanish Gold

In Benton County, Arkansas, between the towns of Gravette and Sulphur Springs near the Missouri border, lies a cave associated with a fascinating legend of hidden gold. Originally called Black Cave, it is now a minor tourist attraction, advertised on a nearby billboard as "The Spanish Treasure Cave." Not too many years ago, residents of Benton County were eager and curious to know exactly what the cave contained.

One Ozark legend relates that some representatives of the Spanish army made exploratory forays from deep in Mexico up through Texas and into the Oklahoma-Missouri-Arkansas border area. Along the way they robbed and pillaged Indian villages, eventually amassing a large fortune in gold. They arrived in what is now Benton County in midwinter and sought shelter in one of the many limestone caverns found in the region.

The party of nineteen soldiers finally succeeded in locating a cavern that was large enough for both men and horses and faced an area that provided plenty of firewood. Here they would be content to wait out the cold weather as long as necessary. While they remained close to the mouth of the cave, they noted that a passageway ran deep into the mountainside and the light from their modest campfire was not able to penetrate its depths.

A party of about thirty Indians had been trailing the Spaniards for several days. It is believed the Spaniards, after raiding the Indian camp about a week earlier, had stolen several of the tribe's women. Intent on revenge and recapturing their women, the braves had dogged the Spaniards' trail ever since.

During a heavy snowfall one afternoon, one of the Indian scouts spotted the smoke from the soldiers' campfire as it exited a natural vent in the rock above the cave. After scouting the area thoroughly, the Indians made elaborate plans during the night. When dawn broke, they launched a ferocious attack, and for several hours they battled until all the Spaniards were killed. Before they died, however, several of the soldiers carried the gold deep into one of the passageways of the cave and cached it within.

Nothing more was heard of this incident until early in the fall of 1885, when an old Spanish gentleman arrived in Sulphur Springs. He was carrying three ancient parchment maps, each of which contained involved directions on how to reach the cave in which the Spaniards had concealed the gold.

The old man was precise and mannerly in his dealings with the Benton County citizens, and while his command of English was poor, he managed to communicate details of the lost Spanish gold.

He said that a second detachment of soldiers was sent north to ascertain the fate of the first group. They encountered many Indian villages along the way and heard descriptions of raids made by the soldiers as well as of their taking gold and women and killing many warriors. Eventually the second group of soldiers came upon the cave and found the skeletons of their comrades, victims of the Indian massacre. The soldiers explored the cave and discovered a great fortune in gold cached at the back of one of the many long passageways. Since they lacked extra horses or mules to transport the gold, they decided to bury it deep within the cave until they or others could return for it. They spent days filling the chambers and passageways of the cave with dirt in order to discourage others from entering.

The old Spaniard hired two local men, one named Callister and the other named John Harwick, to guide him into the woods in search of the cave. For several days they searched, with no luck.

One day the Spaniard was able to make the two guides understand that the cave they were looking for had positioned at its entrance a large rock with the image of a deer hoof carved on it. After several more days of searching and talking with people who lived in the area, they located a squatter far back in the woods by the name of Rufus Wetzel. Wetzel and his family, which consisted of nine children and a very skinny, tired-looking wife, lived in a poorly constructed log cabin in a remote part of the Ozark Mountains not far from the town of Gravette.

Wetzel said he was aware of such a rock and had seen it many times while hunting in the woods. But he declined to show the men the rock's location and kept asking why they wanted to know. The Spaniard feared that if the mountain man was told information about the treasure in the cave he would try to retrieve it for himself. They tried to bargain with the squatter, offering him unheard-of sums of money for the information, but the more they offered him the more suspicious he became.

One day when Wetzel had disappeared into the woods to hunt deer, Mrs. Wetzel, anxious for the intruders to be on their way, agreed to show them the stone they sought. She led the men deep into the woods about a mile from the cabin and pointed it out.

As they approached the rock, the Spaniard became quite excited. Without a doubt this was the stone described in the ancient Spanish documents. It was very large and required the assistance of several more men before it could be removed from the opening of the cave.

Once the great rock was removed, they saw that the interior of the cavern was indeed filled from bottom to top with dirt that had apparently been carried in. The Spaniard hired the same men to excavate the fill dirt from the passage. Eager for wages, the men set to the task. After several days of work that they had removed only a small portion of the dirt, but they were happy to continue their labors, for the Spaniard was paying them well.

As dirt was removed from the passageway, the diggers found bits and pieces of Spanish armor and weapons, lending credence to the notion that the Spanish had indeed visited this cave at an earlier time.

The days passed into weeks and still the men continued to dig. The more fill dirt they encountered, the more convinced they were that some great treasure was concealed at the end. Why else would anyone go to so much trouble?

During the excavation, the Spanish gentleman came down with a serious fever and had to be confined to a pallet. For a time he lay in the shade of a nearby tree, directing the excavation, but it soon became clear he was suffering from a severe case of pneumonia and it did not appear he would live much longer. Eventually he informed the diggers that he needed to go south to Texas where the climate was much warmer and more hospitable to a man in his condition. He left enough money to pay the men for their continued digging, and as he rode away he told them he would make contact with them as soon as possible.

The old man gathered up his maps and, along with all the old pieces of armor and weapons that had been removed from the cave, packed them into his wagon. Before leaving, he explained to the men that once they broke through the fill dirt they would find that the cave branched out into several corridors, each heading in a different direction, and that the treasure was supposed to be concealed in one of them. He reassured the diggers that when he was well he would return and they would all share in the treasure. With that, he departed.

The men continued to dig for several more days but soon tired of the labor. They divided the money that had been left and promised each other they would resume the excavation if he ever returned. The Spaniard was never heard from again, and the story of the lost Spanish gold cached in the old cave passed into Ozark folklore.

In 1922, a Benton County man named Parkins traveled to Oklahoma to search for work. His journey took him to the little settlement of Paul's Valley in the south-central part of the state, where he found employment as a carpenter. He soon made friends with a fellow worker who asked him many questions about Arkansas.

Eventually the talk turned to caves in the Arkansas Ozarks,

and the new friend told Parkins he knew a story about an old Spanish treasure cave up near the Arkansas-Missouri border. Parkins, having been raised on the local folklore of the Spanish cave, asked the man how he came to know of the legend.

The friend told Parkins that during the winter of 1886, a very sick old Spanish gentleman stopped at Paul's Valley on his way to Texas. The man was seriously ill and was taken in by the friend's father, who intended to nurse him back to health. He became sicker and it was soon clear that he would not live much longer. On his deathbed he confided to the family that he had some old maps that showed the way to a Spanish treasure in a cave in Arkansas. If anything happened to him, he asked, could they please send the maps to an address in Madrid, Spain? The family agreed, but the man died before he was able to provide them with the address.

The friend took Parkins out to the old Paul's Valley cemetery and showed him the Spaniard's grave. A rotted wooden marker bore the barely readable inscription "Age Unknown. A Traveler From Spain."

When Parkins inquired about the maps, the friend said that they had remained in the family's possession for a long time but that he no longer knew where they were.

Sometime around 1900, one George Dunbar arrived in Gravette from somewhere in the East. Dunbar claimed to have yet another set of Spanish maps and documents that identified the same cave as one that contained a great Spanish treasure. He also said his information stated exactly where the gold was concealed inside the cave.

Dunbar thought it would be a simple matter of going to the cave, following the map, retrieving the gold, and walking out. He did not reckon with the many tons of fill dirt stuffing the passageways.

He examined the cave and observed the work of previous diggers. He was amazed at the number of small passageways that extended out from the main corridor in various directions, many of them still filled with dirt, but he thought the job of removing the fill was only a temporary barrier between him and the vast fortune in Spanish gold he knew to be awaiting him.

Dunbar hired a crew to continue the excavation of the cave. When he thought the work was proceeding too slowly, he had his men install small-gauge railroad tracks through many of the passageways, tracks on which ran ore carts to speed the removal of the dirt. He excavated farther and farther into the many branches, only to find more openings filled with yet more dirt.

He awoke each morning believing that day would be the one in which he located the gold, but each evening he went to bed disappointed. For several years he supervised the excavation of the cave until he eventually ran out of money. Never healthy, Dunbar allowed his failure and subsequent depression to weigh heavily on his mind and within a matter of weeks he died, an old, broken man who was never able to realize his dream.

Within a year after Dunbar's death, a W.W. Knight picked up the excavation of the cave. He employed an even larger crew and extended the tracks deeper into the cave. His men often worked round-the-clock, but even with that Knight came no closer to the gold than any of the others who searched. He quit his excavation in 1918. Over the next few decades men tried to take up the excavation where others left off, but all were unsuccessful.

Longtime residents of the Gravette area can recall their grandparents and great-grandparents telling of a great earthquake that shook the region in 1812. The tremor fractured much of the thinly-layered limestone rock that makes up this portion of the Ozark Mountains, and as a result many of the caverns in this area are prone to cave-ins. Some suggest that this is what happened in the old Spanish Cave in Benton County—that a cave-in collapsed portions of the cavern system, forever concealing the Spaniards' gold deep within the interior. Many also believe that much of the dirt that was excavated had not been placed in the cavern by the Spaniards, but filtered in from above through the many fractures in the rock.

Over the years fortunes have been spent in attempting to locate and retrieve the hidden gold of the Spaniards, but the treasure remains hidden, concealed deep within the mysterious cave.

The Madre Vena Ore Cache

One of the most talked-about lost treasure caches in the Arkansas Ozarks is associated with the Madre Vena Cave. Though some of the stories refer to the "Madre Vena Mine," it is probably not a mine at all but a natural cavern in which gold and silver ore was concealed over 130 years ago. In any case, many firmly believe that somewhere in some deep subterranean chamber in the Ozark Mountains lies a fortune waiting for the searcher who can locate it.

The legends and tales of Spaniards operating gold and silver mines in the Ozark Mountains are numerous, and so much evidence has been discovered that that notion is hard to disregard. The Spanish explorers, under the leadership of De Soto, virtually littered the Ozark landscape with tools, weapons, armor, and other artifacts of their culture.

During the peak of the Spanish exploration and mining in the Ozark Mountains, great quantities of the gold and silver taken from the mines would be loaded onto mules and burros and transported out of the mountains toward the southeast. A large company of well-armed soldiers would escort this ore-laden pack train to Florida, where it would in turn be shipped to the motherland. At other times, great caravans carrying remarkable fortunes in precious minerals would travel from deep in the Ozark Mountains to the seat of government in Mexico. The Spanish royalty who resided in Mexico, after receiving such a load of wealth from remote Arkansas, would normally organize another expedition to return for more of the same. These return expeditions would be amply outfitted and often supplied with hundreds of Mexican laborers.

As the years passed and Spanish influence in the New World decreased, the mines in the Ozarks were abandoned and the soldiers and most of the miners returned to Mexico. Some, however, remained in the Ozark Mountains and continued mining gold and silver. Many took Indian wives, and for several generations they and their descendants continued to dig ore from the intrusive rock formations hidden beneath the thick layers of Ozark limestone. As late as the mid-nineteenth century, small groups of Mexicans were believed to be still working in the mines in some of the more remote sections of the Ozarks.

One such group, a foursome led by a man named Manuel Alarcón, had small but continuous successes excavating gold and silver from several different locations in the mountains. After several years of mining, they had accumulated an impressive fortune, but as they transported their wealth from mine to mine and camp to camp on their mules, they came to believe this practice was unwise because of the numerous bandits who frequented the area, and decided to cache their fortune while they mined for more. They searched for a site that was remote and would offer security.

Finally they came upon a cave in northwestern Arkansas close to where the Arkansas-Missouri border is now. Researchers believe the cave is approximately ten miles north of Bentonville and that, while the entrance is in Arkansas, the underground passages extend beneath the border into Missouri.

The four Mexicans examined the cave, explored its many and intricate passageways for two days, and finally located a large chamber that seemed adequate for storing their fortune. Legend claims that the passageway into this chamber was especially low and narrow, and that the four men had somehow managed to wedge a huge oval limestone slab into the entrance, effectively sealing it. In front of the slab they stacked rocks and dirt from the cavern floor, thus further disguising the opening from anyone who chanced to enter and explore the cave. Following this,

41

the Mexicans camped outside the entrance to the cave for several days as they discussed plans to journey to a distant site to mine for more ore. One of the men suggested they name the cave *Madre Vena*—"mother lode." They agreed.

During the evening meal of the second day after caching the ore, Manuel Alarcón proposed that they make a map to the cave. The men carved detailed directions into a thin, wide slab of limestone they found nearby. Included on the map were prominent landmarks in the vicinity, important trails, and the location of the Madre Vena Cave. Unable to agree on where to hide the map, they finally turned in for the night.

Just before dawn the next day, Alarcón arose from his bedroll and slew his three comrades. By the light of the moon, he dug three graves and buried the bodies—lowering the limestone map into one of the graves along with the corpse. Carefully and efficiently, he filled each of the three graves, piled stones across the top of them, and erected wooden markers, each one carved with the name of a dead comrade.

Then he prayed aloud over the graves and conducted a brief funeral service for his former partners.

What possessed Manuel Alarcón to murder his three lifelong friends has puzzled people for many years. Some say he wanted all the gold and silver for himself and the only way he could get it was to eliminate those with whom he would otherwise have to share. Some say he was simply crazy.

With the sun high in the heavens, Alarcón gathered up the horses and supplies and rode away. He paused at a nearby ridge to regard the final resting place of his fellows. Some distance beyond the graves and in the woods, he could discern the entrance to the Madre Vena Cave.

Alarcón was not seen again for thirty years. It has been said that he roamed the Ozarks, a semi-crazed man who was never able to sleep at night, that he became a hermit and shunned all contact with civilization, and that he continued to work small mines in the Ozarks to add to his already large cache of gold and silver buried within the Madre Vena Cave.

He surfaced three decades later in Pierce City, Missouri, a

small community about twenty miles southeast of Joplin. Alarcón was on his deathbed, suffering from a terrible fever, and could breathe only with great difficulty. While he was being treated by a doctor in Pierce City, he related the entire story of the gold and silver cache in the Madre Vena Cave and told of killing his three friends and burying the map on the stone slab in one of the graves. As best he could, he provided directions to the graves and to the cave. The next morning Manuel Alarcón was dead.

News of the Mexican's ore cache spread throughout the Ozarks during the following weeks, and people came from several states to search for the great wealth in the cave. The Ozark hills and mountains near the Missouri-Arkansas border were crawling with hopeful treasure-hunters for several months, but nothing was ever found.

A few years later, a man familiar with the Madre Vena Cave story undertook a search in a rather remote valley and one that had not received the attention of previous searchers.

After two days of exploring the area, the man discovered three graves in a little glade near the edge of a thick oak and hickory forest. He spent the next few days scouring the woods but was unable to locate a cave that matched the description provided by the dying Alarcón. Presently he returned to the glade and started to dig up the graves. In the second one he discovered the limestone slab with the map chiseled into the surface.

With great difficulty the man raised the stone slab from the grave. Realizing the slab was too large to transport, he copied the map onto a piece of paper. Then he demolished the stone so others could not use it, threw the pieces back into the grave, and refilled it.

Even with the map, the man had no luck in locating the Madre Vena Cave. After two weeks of searching in the area, he abandoned it, never to return.

Several years later, the man passed the map along to a friend named Vanwormer who lived in Afton, Oklahoma. Vanwormer made one or two halfhearted searches for the Madre Vena Cave but never had any luck. Several years later he gave the map to his son, Frank.

Frank Vanwormer was considerably more enthusiastic about the Madre Vena treasure than his father and made several determined forays into the Arkansas Ozarks in search of it. Though he was unsuccessful, he was nevertheless convinced that the treasure was real and that it was only a matter of time before he located it.

Vanwormer eventually learned of the interest of another man from Afton who had also been searching for the Madre Vena treasure for many years. His name was John Koch, and he claimed to have reliable evidence that the cave was in a certain little valley in another remote part of northwest Arkansas.

Vanwormer, Koch, and a third man joined forces and systematically combed the countryside. One day they came upon the graves of the three men killed and buried by Manuel Alarcon. They dug up the graves and discovered the shattered pieces of the stone map. In trying to reconstruct the stone map, they found that several of the broken parts were missing, giving an incomplete picture of the area. It was useless.

Being familiar with Alarcon's story, and knowing that the graves were supposed to be close to the entrance of the lost Madre Vena Cave, the men concentrated their search in a small area east of the three graves.

On the afternoon of the second day they discovered a cave along a low bank of limestone outcrop not far from the graves. The entrance had apparently been disguised with rocks and dirt piled in front of it. In the years since this was done, small trees and shrubs had grown up in the debris, causing it to blend in with the surrounding forest. This was undoubtedly why the opening had been so difficult to detect for so many years.

With some effort the men removed the trees, shrubs, rocks, and debris and found themselves looking into a dark passageway that continued laterally into the side of the hill.

They soon discovered that retrieving the cache was to be no easy task. The cave had numerous passageways—some of them dead ends and others appearing to extend into the mountain forever. The men estimated there were several miles of passage-ways in the cave.

They searched the interior of the cave for a week, but were no closer to retrieving the treasure than they were the day they discovered the opening.

They returned to their homes in Oklahoma for a time to attend to personal business. When the search was resumed several weeks later, the third man elected not to return to the Ozarks, saying he did not believe the treasure existed and that he had neglected his farm long enough.

Vanwormer and Koch continued to explore the cavern. One day while examining a new passageway, they discovered a large, somewhat circular stone slab wedged into what they believed was the opening into a natural chamber. They determined that the stone could not have been placed there naturally and that it must have required the labor of several men to move it.

Using crowbars and levers, they tried to pry the great stone out of the opening, but were unable to dislodge it. On a return visit to the cave, they carried several bundles of dynamite with them. The first charge they set off did nothing but scar the face of the large slab and did not move it at all. They decided to set a larger charge, which also failed to move the slab, but did cause a portion of the roof to weaken and crumble. They then tried an even larger charge of explosive.

Flying rock debris from the third charge struck Koch, injuring him severely. He had to be dragged from the cave and transported to a doctor.

While Koch was recovering, Vanwormer returned to the Madre Vena Cave to examine the results of the latest charge of dynamite. More of the cavern roof had been destroyed, but the stone was still wedged in the same position.

With his injury and the disappointing news about the stone slab, Koch became disheartened and declared he was abandoning his search. Vanwormer, depressed that his partner did not wish to continue, made a few more halfhearted attempts to remove the large stone slab from the hidden passageway but eventually gave up.

As Vanwormer quit the cave, he purposely set off several more dynamite charges, which caused a portion of the cavern roof to collapse and fill in much of the main passageway. His intention was to discourage other searchers.

Around 1915, a man named Enoch Hodges rediscovered the Madre Vena Cave and reportedly began digging through the collapsed rubble that resulted from Vanwormer's dynamite charges. Hodges worked intermittently for five years trying to clear a passageway through the dirt and rock but eventually gave up.

Since the 1920s other attempts to reach the Madre Vena ore cache have been organized, but all have ended in failure.

Today, according to researchers, a small landslide that occurred in the region sometime during the mid-1960s has covered the entrance to the Madre Vena Cave. Once again trees and brush have grown up in the debris that covers the opening, making it difficult to detect. Beyond the covered entrance and the collapsed rubble in the main passageway of the cave, a fortune in gold and silver ore may still be gathering dust in the dark chamber.

Spanish Silver
in Searcy County

During the first decade of the twentieth century a man named Herndon spent considerable time doing some exploratory mining near Silver Hill in Searcy County. Throughout this prospect area he occasionally found traces of silver ore, but never enough to justify any serious large-scale mining.

One day, however, he located a vein of silver that held some promise. Herndon was encouraged to the point of filing a claim and employing a surveyor to locate and mark property lines. The surveyor was a local man, very knowledgeable about the history of the region. As they were walking around the area of the claim, the surveyor told Herndon that not far from where they stood was some evidence of ancient Spanish mining. Intrigued, Herndon asked the surveyor to lead him to the location. About twenty minutes later they arrived at a clearing consisting mainly of exposed bedrock. In the center of the open space was a crater-like excavation ringed by several large mounds of rock debris that had apparently been removed from it. Trees growing out of the old mounds of excavated debris testified to their age.

Sixty years earlier, the surveyor said, a man who identified himself as a Mexican priest had arrived in the area. He claimed he was an emissary from a church in Mexico in which was discovered an aged Spanish map purporting to show the location of a fabulous silver mine in Arkansas. The priest produced the map from a well-made leather case and showed it to several area residents. The map was of heavy parchment on which was crudely sketched a system of trails and the outlines and descriptions of several mountains and hills. Many of the residents recognized the landmarks as being consistent with the Silver Hill environment.

The priest said the information given to him by church officials suggested the map had been constructed by a soldier who had served with De Soto, and indicated a site where a very rich silver deposit had been extensively mined centuries earlier. The map gave the location of the mine in precise degrees of latitude and longitude and was dated 1580.

The brief written description on the ancient map told how great quantities of silver had been taken from a deep shaft carved into the limestone rock of the mountain and smelted down into ingots for ease of transportation back to the Spanish homeland.

The Spaniards were forced to cut short their mining however, because of continued threats from hostile Indians. Recurrent raids and occasional killings reduced the force of Spaniards until they believed it was not safe to remain in the region. For several nights, under cover of darkness, the Spanish miners systematically filled in the shaft. Then they loaded as many of the silver ingots as possible onto mules and abandoned the site. One legend suggests that the Spaniards were overtaken by Indians and all were killed. Another legend says they were pursued for several days by the Indians and battled them often but finally escaped. The existence of the map in the church archives in Mexico suggests there may be some truth to the second legend. In any case, the Spanish apparently never returned to rework the silver mine in the Ozark Mountains.

The surveyor told Herndon that the Mexican priest offered a group of area residents half of the silver remaining in the shaft if they would excavate the many tons of rock the Spanish had used to fill it. An agreement was made, and several men neglected their farms while they pursued the dream of a fortune in silver.

As the excavation commenced, it became evident that the men were digging into an old vertical mine shaft that had been filled in. After several days of digging, they had removed about twelve feet of fill from the wide shaft. Soon thereafter, they encountered a huge limestone slab that had somehow been wedged into the shaft and firmly secured, preventing any further penetration into the old mine. The diggers judged that it must have taken twenty men to place the large rock in that position. After several unsuccessful attempts at removing it, they finally blasted through the slab using several charges of dynamite.

Once the debris from the blasted rock was cleared away, the men could see that the shaft leveled off to a more horizontal angle, and on its floor they found numerous mining tools of Spanish origin. The workers also discovered several molds into which hot metal had evidently been poured to form ingots. However, even after searching thoroughly, they found no seam of silver. A curious question presented itself—if all of the silver had been mined, why was the long shaft so elaborately sealed?

A mining engineering firm from Kansas City was hired to examine the site and decide the potential for the existence of silver. Like the diggers before them, the consultants had no luck in locating a vein of ore in the shaft. They did find evidence that this had indeed been a working silver mine at one time, but they still could not resolve the question of why the shaft had been filled in. On this same consulting visit, the Kansas City company discovered several small veins of silver in the hills nearby, and started mining operations that lasted for several years.

The Mexican priest, discouraged at not being able to locate any of the wealth alluded to in the ancient document, returned to his home country.

Herndon continued to prospect for and mine some small amounts of silver, but he also eventually abandoned the area.

As the years passed, the other silver mines in the region were worked out and the Kansas City company closed them and moved away. Shortly thereafter, an old man named Grinder moved into one of the abandoned mine buildings, squatting on the land on which the old Spanish mine was located.

Grinder was an eccentric who had lived in the nearby hills all his life and survived mostly by hunting and trapping. He occasionally did odd jobs for some of the local farmers, but most people considered him a little crazy, and because he was rather coarse and unkempt, shunned him. Soon, however, the talk around the county was that old man Grinder was digging in the old Spanish shaft in the hope of locating the lost vein of silver. Laughter and jokes directed at the old man were the usual response to his mining, for no one seriously believed the old coot would find anything.

After working in the shaft for several weeks, Grinder ordered and paid for some mining equipment that was delivered from Little Rock to the Silver Hill site. Area citizens were baffled as to where Grinder obtained money to pay for what amounted to thousands of dollars' worth of sophisticated machinery.

Shunning the town, Grinder spent all his time out at the mine, apparently working intently in the deepest part of the shaft for many hours at a time. Visitors to the old mine were ordered away at the point of a shotgun.

Within a year, Grinder abandoned his mining endeavor and sold all the equipment. To the surprise of many, he shortly thereafter purchased a 120-acre farm in a neighboring county, stocked it with a large herd of fine cattle, and paid for everything with cash.

Those who ventured into the old Spanish shaft after it was abandoned by Grinder told of how a completely new passageway had been opened and penetrated deep into the rock for several dozen yards.

Had old man Grinder discovered the long-concealed vein of silver ore that the Spaniards had gone to so much trouble to hide? Evidently he found something that encouraged him to dig and remove tons of rock singlehandedly. Whatever he found, old man Grinder was not telling, and he apparently took his secret to his grave.

The Lost Tabor Mine

Tabor was a poor man who lived a hermit's life in the woods and mountains near the town of St. Joe in Searcy County. Slightly crippled and inflicted with a speech impediment, he was well known to the townsfolk. The few times he would come into town to purchase provisions, he always paid for them with pure silver ore. When asked about the origin of the silver, Tabor would cackle a toothless laugh and his tall skinny frame would launch into an awkward dance while he teased the locals that they would never be able to locate his mine.

Sometimes people tried to follow Tabor back into the hills where he lived, but he always managed to elude the trackers after leading them for miles in circles through the dark woods.

Near the end of 1865, Tabor was no longer seen around St. Joe, and as he was an elderly man, people assumed he had met his end alone in the remote and often hostile wilderness of the Ozark Mountains. Now and then somebody would venture into the Tomahawk Creek region in search of Tabor's silver mine, but no one ever claimed to have found it. Most who entered the region returned telling stories of the dark, close forest that seemed to be haunted. People searched for the silver mine off and on for nearly fifty years, but the story of the eccentric old man and his wealth was eventually forgotten.

Hulce Taylor owned some land along Tomahawk Creek and managed to earn a respectable living by farming the bottoms and raising some cattle. One morning in 1924 he took his young daughter with him as he set out in search of two cows that had strayed from the main herd.

After about half a day of searching, the farmer and daughter found themselves walking alongside a remote stretch of overgrown trail that paralleled Tomahawk Creek. Taylor had never been to this part of the woods before and he proceeded cautiously. Here the forest of tall oak and hickory was very dense, and the trail was more like a tunnel than a passage through the woods. Little light penetrated the thick forest canopy to reach the ground. There was moisture everywhere and the area had the pungent smell of rotting vegetation. Just beyond their range of vision, deep in the woods, small unseen forest creatures skittered through the underbrush.

The little girl told her father she was frightened and wanted to return home, but Taylor coaxed her into going on. The farther they walked the narrower the little valley became, until it seemed as if the very walls would close in on them. Thick dense vines grew from the forest floor up to the tops of the sheer limestone cliffs.

Presently they arrived at a portion of the valley where several large trees had been blown down, making further passage difficult. Taylor presumed the toppled trees were a result of a violent storm that had struck the area a few days before.

Just as Taylor decided to return back up the trail, he noticed that the dense vines that had covered one portion of a cliff had been torn away, probably by high winds. There, near the center of the recently exposed cliff, was the entrance to an old mine.

He later described the mine as containing a rich vein of silver ore so pure it could be easily dug out with a pocketknife. When neighbors began to ask too many questions about the mine and the silver, Taylor resorted to silence. Soon he refused to speak of the mine in front of anyone, even his own children.

Taylor's farm continued to prosper, even when other farmers were having hard times, and many neighbors believed he was secretly mining the silver from the old shaft. No records exist to verify whether he did, and Taylor's descendants have been unable to provide any information.

From the geographic location and description of the shaft Taylor accidentally happened upon, it is likely the Lost Tabor

Mine. In any case, it has apparently been lost again and, in spite of several organized attempts to relocate it, remains lost.

Lost Aztec Mine in Franklin County?

In legends of lost mines and buried treasures in the Ozarks, one sometimes hears vague references to gold mines operated by the Aztec Indians. This notion is remarkable, because the Aztecs' homeland is hundreds of miles south in Mexico. It seems unlikely that members of that Meso-American tribe would make the long journey to the Ozarks to mine gold, but the legends and folktales persist. Many dismiss the stories as so much nonsense, saying there has never been any physical evidence of the presence of Aztec Indians in the Ozarks.

However, for years mysterious petroglyphs have been discovered in remote portions of the Ozarks. The origins of these writings on the stone are clearly prehistoric, and several scholars suggest that they bear some similarity to Aztec symbols, but, they hasten to point out, that is mere conjecture and not to be taken as proof.

In 1986 a remarkable discovery was made on Wolverton Mountain, a flat-topped narrow sandstone ridge in northern Conway County. Several farmers and ranchers living on the mountain were battling a fire and had plowed a firebreak between the forest and a grass field. As a plow cut through a shallow layer of soil, it kicked up a small carved stone figure of a human being. Its style was unmistakably Meso-American, strikingly similar to that of carvings unearthed in ancient Aztec excavations in Mexico. Several experts who have seen the stone figure have tentatively identified it as being Indian, most likely

Aztec.

While this stone carving may not prove Aztec visitation in the Ozarks, it certainly opens the door to speculation that such an event might indeed have occurred.

One man who resides in Franklin County has reason to believe that the Aztecs visited that region long ago. O.P. VanBrunt, a septuagenarian who lives in Mulberry, has been searching for a lost gold mine in the Ozark Mountains for many years. He has been passionately pursuing the notion that there is a fortune in gold hidden away in a tunnel in a hill in the northeastern part of the county.

VanBrunt's father also searched many years for the tunnel, starting in 1918. Like other residents of the area, he always referred to it as the Lost Spanish Mine and associated it with the mining of Spanish explorers who visited this region with De Soto.

Arkansas legend says that the Spanish encountered Aztec Indians mining gold in the region when they arrived. Some claim that the Spaniards drove the Indians out, while others believe all of the Aztecs were slain by the conquistadores. In either case, the Spanish apparently took over the rich mining operation that was begun by the Aztecs and worked it for several years.

It is told that the Spanish remained in the area until the war with France broke out and that there was a possibility it might extend to the Americas. Fearing their mine and gold would be seized, the Spaniards stored the wealth of several years of mining deep in the excavated tunnel, sealed it, and left mysterious writings and symbols on cliff faces and rock outcrops in the region to guide them back to the mine when they were able to return. They never did.

The story of the mine, however, lived on in the oral tradition, and when this region was being settled in the latter part of the last century, occasional forays into the Ozarks in search of the mine took place.

In 1915, a local physician named Tobe Hill became fascinated with the stories about the lost Aztec mine worked by the Spanish. Hill once related a story about an interesting encounter with an aged Spaniard traveling through the Ozarks. The old man, obviously tired and hungry, stopped by the Hill residence asking directions. Hill invited him to stay for dinner and learned that he was seeking the Lost Spanish Mine. The Spaniard said that he learned of the mine's existence from relatives in his homeland who had provided him with information about the symbols and writings that were supposed to lead to the site of the hidden mine. As he sketched several of these symbols, the physician recalled seeing such drawings and scrawlings on many limestone outcrops several miles north of his farm.

The next morning the Spaniard thanked Hill and bade him farewell as he walked off into the mountains. He was never seen again in the Ozarks.

In 1918, Hill formed the Louisiana Mining Company and, with several associates, sought the legendary mine for four years.

O.P. VanBrunt, whose father was associated with the Louisiana Mining Company, remembers traveling with his father by covered wagon to a remote part of the Ozarks as a six-year-old. He and his father lived at the site for two weeks, digging in likely places for the opening to the elusive tunnel. At one point in their digging, the elder VanBrunt found a rock speckled with gold. He recovered enough ore from the rock to fashion two wedding bands.

VanBrunt lacked the opportunity to return to the diggings during the succeeding decades, but his interest in the Lost Spanish Mine never waned. In 1973 he resumed searching for the cache on McElroy Mountain in the northeastern part of Franklin County. Many caves and several man-made tunnels have been found in the mountain, and VanBrunt is convinced that the stored wealth of the Spaniards and Aztecs lies concealed within.

Jesse Jones, who owns most of McElroy Mountain and leases the digging rights to VanBrunt, is also convinced of the existence of the mine and the hidden treasure. Jones, in fact, believes he actually discovered the entrance to what he calls the "Doc Hill Mine." He said it is on the western side of the mountain near the

Mulberry River. The tunnel, according to Jones, measures six feet by six feet and penetrates the mountain to a depth of nearly 150 feet. Here and there in the tunnel can be found the remains of ancient timbers once used for shoring.

Jones claims to have found a small wheel fashioned from gold near the mountain. He said he sent it with a man to have it assayed but it never came back. Jones also claims to have panned gold flakes from a small stream that flows close to the entrance of the tunnel.

Both VanBrunt and Jones are convinced that the ancient writings found on the bare rock walls in the area tell of the gold's location, but no one has yet been able to interpret their meaning.

VanBrunt said McElroy Mountain is remarkably different from other mountains in the area. The rock layers of McElroy Mountain have a rusty tinge, and when the sun is at a certain angle they take on a coloring as red as blood. According to local legend, the mountain was stained forever by the blood of the slain Aztecs and is cursed, never to give up its fortune in gold secreted deep within.

The Lost Tunnel of Gold

One warm summer afternoon in the mid-1960s, Ralph Mayes paid his daily visit to his father-in-law, who was recuperating in the Washington County Hospital. He brought a small bag of items his father-in-law needed from home as well as a paperback western to read while he was laid up.

Mayes's father-in-law shared his hospital room with a man named Alvin Bishop. Bishop was recovering from a heart attack, and as he had come to know young Ralph Mayes, he also looked forward to his visits.

Today Mayes asked Bishop what had brought on his heart attack and heard a remarkable story of a lost gold mine in the Boston Mountain region of the Ozarks.

Alvin Bishop said that he had come into possession of a very old parchment map that purported to show the location of a hidden tunnel wherein large, thick veins of pure gold could be found. The map had been given to his grandfather by local Indians many years earlier and was handed down to his father and then to him. It was full of cryptic figures and symbols and the writing was definitely Spanish. Though the map was difficult to interpret, Bishop, along with his father, recognized many of the landforms indicated on it and decided to search for the treasure.

The two men hiked many miles through the Ozarks over the next few years in search of the hidden tunnel. While many of the landmarks noted on the map matched those in the territory through which they searched, the men remained frustrated at not being able to understand many of the symbols, which allegedly showed the exact location of the tunnel.

Then in 1963 they found it. They drove to the old Sunnydale schoolhouse some three miles east of the town of Winslow on State Highway 71 and from there followed an old, seldom-used dirt road in a more or less southerly direction. The road ended at a ridge known locally as Piney Point, where the men had to leave their vehicle and walk a narrow trail, eventually coming into a valley on the west side of the ridge. They followed a small stream in the valley for some distance, looking for a large flat rock near a large oak tree shown on the old map. The entrance to the tunnel was supposed to be beneath the rock.

With great difficulty, Alvin Bishop and his father succeeded in shifting the rock just enough to reveal the opening of a vertical tunnel, which had obviously been excavated with primitive mining tools centuries earlier. The shaft was square, and along two opposing walls thick veins of gold ran into the shaft as far as the two could see.

Alvin Bishop had exhausted himself in moving the huge rock and, before taking a much-needed rest, he decided to climb into the tunnel in order to evaluate the wealth that lay before him. With great difficulty he lowered himself into the vertical tunnel and, bracing his back against one wall and his feet against the other, started to descend the shaft. As he exerted himself, he suffered a heart attack, and it was only with great difficulty that his father was able to remove him from the ancient mine and bring him to the Washington County Hospital.

Mayes was fascinated by Bishop's story and determined to learn more about the old Spanish mine. Each day he looked forward to visiting with Bishop, and soon the two men entered into an agreement to go to the mine, extract the gold, and share in the wealth. Bishop would provide directions to the mine, and Mayes would provide the labor.

Mayes and Bishop talked several more times before Bishop regained his strength and was discharged from the hospital. Several more meetings at the Bishop home resulted in a plan to journey to the isolated valley west of Piney Point and from there to the tunnel of gold.

While Bishop was preparing equipment for the expedition he suffered another heart attack. He was dead before he was able to receive medical attention.

Several weeks after Bishop's death, his widow turned the old Spanish map over to Mayes. Since Bishop never explained the meanings of the various signs and symbols on the map, Mayes could not interpret any of it. Furthermore, as he was totally unfamiliar with the Ozark Mountains east of Winslow, he had no idea what to look for. To compound the problem, he could find no geographic designation of a Piney Point. Baffled and frustrated, he soon lost the desire to search for the tunnel of gold.

Though unable to find it, Ralph Mayes firmly believed in the existence of the tunnel. He was convinced that Alvin Bishop had located the shaft and had actually entered it. Mayes believed that not being able to locate the tunnel had likely cost him the opportunity of becoming a millionaire. For Alvin Bishop, finding the tunnel ultimately cost him his life.

King's River Silver

Prior to the Indian removal initiated by the United States government in the 1830s, the Ozark Mountain region in the northwestern part of Arkansas was home to several tribes who lived in relative peace and harmony. They grew corn, beans, and squash along the river bottoms and ran cattle and horses where good grazing could be found. This agricultural bounty was supplemented with hunting and fishing from the abundant woods and streams. The King's River region in what is now Carroll County offered an abundance of such good living, so it is little wonder that when a few white settlers moved into the area the Indians welcomed them openly and fully.

Jasper Combs and his family were among the first whites to share in this bounty. Around 1820, Combs established a small farmstead along one side of the river and began to grow crops and raise livestock. He became good friends with the Indians he met in the area. They occasionally shared meals and engaged in trade. Combs and the Indians hunted and fished together and helped each other build cabins, plow fields, and cooperate in the raising of livestock. Combs's children played with the Indian children, and life in the valley was good.

During Combs's many dealings with the Indian residents of the valley, he noticed that several of them wore arm bands, necklaces, and other jewelry that appeared to be fashioned from pure silver. He asked where they found the metal but they always steered the conversation toward other topics. Once, when having dinner with an Indian family, Combs noticed that even some of the cooking utensils were made from silver.

With the passing months Combs's curiosity grew keener. One afternoon as he and one of the tribe elders were returning from a hunting trip, he asked again where the silver came from.

The elder explained to Combs that the source of the silver was an old mine whose location was well known to the Indians but was kept a carefully guarded secret from others. Any member of the tribe who revealed the location of the mine would be dealt a swift and certain death at the hands of his fellows.

Having great respect for the traditions of the Indians as well as placing a great value on them as friends, Combs promised never to concern himself with the matter again.

Around the beginning of the 1830s, the federal government undertook a project to remove the Native Americans from their farms and homesteads in the Ozark Mountains and resettle them on lands in the West. When the people of the King's River area were being moved, an arrangement was made with United States government officials to hold a certain parcel of land in their name and to let them return to it from time to time. The Indians claimed it was holy ground and that their ancestors were buried on it, but Jasper Combs believed it was the site of their silver mine.

Jesse Combs, a son of Jasper Combs, recalled times when the Indians returned to the area. Arriving from the Oklahoma settlements in horse-drawn wagons, they would stop at the Combs' homestead to await more arrivals and then proceed to the assigned parcel of land, where they would remain for several days before returning to Oklahoma Territory. When they left, their wagons were loaded down with pure silver.

According to Jesse Combs, the Indians made regular trips to the area until the Civil War. As a result of the hostile presence of Union and Confederate soldiers throughout this part of the Arkansas Ozarks, the Indians stayed away, and by the time the Civil War ended they had ceased coming to the King's River area.

Lester Combs, a son of Jesse and grandson of Jasper, was a longtime resident of Springdale, Arkansas, and liked to tell a story he had heard from his father. He said his father, Jesse, once met a young Indian while working in a sawmill near Kingston, just up the King's River from the old Combs farmstead. The boy was knowledgeable about the special parcel of land allotted to the Indians during the removal phase during the 1830s and said that his elderly grandfather, who lived on an Indian reservation in Oklahoma, probably knew the whereabouts of the ancient silver mine that was believed to be on the Indian land.

Jesse Combs, intrigued by the potential existence of wealth in the area, arranged for the boy to bring his aged grandfather to the area to see if the old silver mine could be located.

When the grandfather arrived, Combs and the young boy took him to the Indian allotment. The old Indian pointed out many familiar landmarks he remembered as a youth nearly sixty years earlier. He reminisced about people, places, and events from which he had long been separated by time and geography, but his recollections convinced Combs he was indeed intimate with the area.

He finally asked about the silver mine. The aged man thought quietly for several minutes. Slowly, he turned toward Combs and told how, as a young boy, he helped dig silver out of the ancient mine and load it into leather packs. He recalled how they had to crawl on hands and knees far into a tunnel in the side of a mountain to retrieve the silver. They had to carry several torches because it was a long way to the silver and they stayed in the mine most of the day.

The old Indian then repeated the penalty for exposing the location of the sacred mine. At that point, he seemed to hesitate about trying to locate the silver, but finally decided it was time for the wealth to be used for the good of the Indians. He agreed to show the mine to Combs.

For several weeks they explored the area and found many strange carvings and signs on the rocks and trees. The old man continued to find familiar landmarks but appeared to be disoriented with regard to distance and direction.

Combs was growing impatient and tried to push the Indian to remember, but the old man finally gave up and said he wished to return to the reservation in Oklahoma. At first Combs believed the old Indian was reluctant to reveal the location of the silver mine because he feared the punishment awaiting him should he tell. But eventually he came to believe that the old man simply could not remember.

In the years that followed, Combs explored the area of the old Indian land allotment many times in search of some indication of the silver mine, but he was never successful.

The Buried Treasure of Mill Ford Cave

The year was 1825 and the last of a large group of Indians was being removed from their communities around what are now Benton, Madison, and Carroll counties in northwestern Arkansas. Mounted United States soldiers were overseeing the removal and providing escort for the caravans of Indians to resettlement points a few days' ride to the west.

The Indians consisted primarily of members of the Cherokee, Choctaw, and Osage tribes, and their removal was brought about as a result of complaints from some of the more affluent landowners in the area who claimed that the Indians represented a threat to decent, hard-working white settlers. They lobbied government authorities to remove the Native Americans to the newly established territory that was to become Oklahoma. Other white settlers in the Ozarks—those who had lived in friendship with the Indians for many years—correctly viewed the removal as an attempt by wealthy landowners to procure the newly vacated farms and homesteads. In any case, Vice President John C. Calhoun orchestrated a treaty that determined the eventual removal of hundreds of Indians from the area.

Many of the white settlers helped their Indian friends during the move. From throughout the hills and valleys of the Ozarks came entire families who participated in the packing and loading of wagons and driving livestock to their friends' new home in the West.

On their way through the Ozarks, the caravan of Indians, white settlers, and soldiers arrived at Mill Ford, a well-known crossing on the White River. The ford, near the present boundary between Benton and Carroll counties, is now covered by the waters of Beaver Lake.

As a large herd of cattle was being driven across Mill Ford, an old Indian watched from astride his horse on a nearby bank. On the horse next to him was one of the white settlers helping in the move, a longtime friend of the old Indian.

As the last of the cattle entered the river, the old Indian pointed to a high bluff some distance downriver and told his friend an intriguing tale of buried treasure that was connected with it.

Many generations earlier, he related, a large detachment of Spaniards was traveling through this portion of the Ozarks. All of the Spaniards were soldiers and they were escorting several ponderous oxcarts, each filled with silver ingots. Indian legend tells that the Spaniards were transporting silver they had mined somewhere deep in Texas to a river port on the Mississippi from where the wealth was to be rafted to the Gulf, loaded onto a sailing vessel, and from there carried to Spain.

The Spaniards had great difficulty crossing the rugged Ozarks during the rainy season. Many of the creeks were too swollen to ford; the trails were muddy and slick; the huge and heavy oxcarts, so efficient in crossing the prairies, were clumsy and hard to handle in the uneven terrain of the mountains. They often got stuck in the deep mud, and many hours were wasted in extracting them. To add to these problems, the Spaniards became lost in this new country and had been roughly circling the same area for several days.

One rainy afternoon while trying to cross at Mill Ford, the Spaniards were attacked by a large band of Indians that seemed to appear out of nowhere. Though greatly outnumbered, the Spaniards defended themselves fiercely, but the outcome was inevitable: most Spaniards were killed outright during the fighting, and the few who survived the onslaught were subjected to horrible tortures and killed, and their bodies were thrown in the river.

The Indians gathered up the vast fortune in silver ingots, crossed the river, and proceeded downstream to the high limestone bluff, heading for a cave whose narrow entrance was behind the bluff. Once there, they carried the ingots inside and stacked them along one wall near the entrance. The low narrow opening was sealed and covered over with forest debris.

The old Indian relating the story said that many years passed and the Indians forgot about the cache of silver bars in the cave. As far as he knew, he said, the bars were never removed; it is believed they are still stacked along one wall just inside the low entrance. The story of the hidden treasure thrilled young Indians in the area for generations, and the white settlers accepted the tale as part of local folklore.

In the early 1920s, however, something happened that caused area residents to take the old tale a bit more seriously.

Two young men were traveling along the old trail that passed close to the area in which the hidden entrance to the treasure cave was believed to exist. It had been raining hard all day and all the previous night, and the men were having difficulty negotiating the slick path. Not wishing to continue walking along the muddy trail and anxious to get out of the rain, the two found temporary shelter under a nearby tree.

As they huddled there, one of the men pointed toward two dull, gleaming objects just barely sticking out of the ground some twenty yards beyond where they were crouched. When the rain finally subsided, they walked over to the curious objects and discovered them to be two silver ingots partially buried in the soil.

The men dug the silver bars out of the ground and within the week carried them to nearby Fayetteville, where they were assayed. The men were told the two bars displayed an "exceptionally good grade" of silver ore.

Believing they might have accidentally discovered the long-lost treasure cave of the Indians, the two men returned to the area. Unfortunately, the heavy rains of the previous week had eroded away much of the soil from one part of the hillside and deposited it in another, completely rearranging the topography. Several trees, including the one the men had huddled under the week before, had been uprooted and carried down the slope to be deposited in a narrow gully below. For several days the two men searched for the entrance to the cave but were never able to locate the exact point where they dug up the silver ingots.

News of the discovery of the silver bars spread throughout the area, and soon the bluff fronting the White River downstream from the Mill Ford was alive with treasure hunters. Several enterprising individuals tried to sink shafts from the top of the bluff in the hope of penetrating the cavern they knew to exist somewhere deep in the rock, but none was successful.

On the face of the steep bluff overlooking the river a cave opening can be seen. This is known locally as Mill Ford Cave. It is believed that this entrance leads to the back side of the bluff where the treasure is believed to be cached. Several people have entered this cave, but a jumble of rock debris in one of the passages, resulting from an ancient cave-in, has impeded them.

The elusive rear entrance to Mill Ford Cave is still searched for today. It is believed the rising lake waters did not cover it. A group of treasure hunters recently spent several days in the area using metal detectors in the hope of locating some evidence of the cache of silver ingots, but their sensitive instruments remained silent.

Lost Silver Mine
near Huntsville

In 1936, one of the most bizarre trials ever to be held in the state of Arkansas took place at the Madison County courthouse in Huntsville. Two local men were being tried for counterfeiting hundreds of dollars' worth of silver coins and passing them throughout the area. The counterfeiting scheme was discovered only when a sharp-eyed banker noticed that a coin given to him by one of the men was slightly thicker than one from the United States mint.

Huntsville is in the northwestern part of Arkansas in the southern Ozarks. Deep, shaded canyons and densely wooded mountains have long made this area a haven for outlaws, bootleggers, and whiskey still operators. These days, one finds mostly pulpwood loggers and farmers, and while stories of lost or buried treasures will come up in conversation occasionally, most residents of this county have little memory of the counterfeiting trial of nearly sixty-five years earlier.

The two Huntsville counterfeiters were arrested without incident. When the time arrived for them to make their statements during the trial, they both freely admitted that they had, in fact, been involved in the making of bogus silver dollars from ore they extracted from a secret mine. The story they told generated one of the most intensive searches for a lost silver mine ever to occur in the state of Arkansas, a search that continues today.

The two men claimed they had initially learned of the existence of the silver mine many years earlier from an old man named Elliot. Elliot was not living at the time of the trial but it is believed he took the two men to the mine and showed them how to retrieve the ore. Several Huntsville residents said that old man Elliot was himself known to have counterfeited silver dollars during the Civil War in this area, and passed his skills on to the two Huntsville men. He showed the two how to fashion the wooden molds used in forming the images on the fake coins.

Both men stated they dug pure silver from an old mine within a half-day's walk from the Madison County courthouse. They carried the silver ore in canvas packs to a secluded site in Bear Creek Hollow, some ten miles northeast of Huntsville and near the small community of Forum. Bear Creek Hollow was remote enough that it was seldom visited by anyone, except possibly the whiskey still operators and customers rumored in local folklore. The hollow seemed like an ideal location for the counterfeiters' activities.

Some students of Arkansas history believe that the men actually mined the silver from somewhere in Bear Creek Hollow and made up the story of its location near Huntsville to throw searchers off the trail. They point to an obscure historical reference to the fact that silver was, in fact, discovered in Bear Creek Hollow in 1886.

Once the men had accumulated a sufficient amount of the ore, they melted it down and rolled it out into thin sheets about the width of a coin. Then they set a mold atop the sheet of silver and hammered it with a mallet, forming a coin and imposing an image on one side. They turned over the coin, hammered another image onto the other side, grooved the edges of the newly made coin by hand, and shortly thereafter placed it into circulation.

Those who have claimed to have seen the wooden molds used by the two Huntsville men testified they were well-made and that the images stamped onto the counterfeit coins were difficult to distinguish from real ones. An analysis of the silver content of one of the coins revealed that they contained a higher quantity of silver than those minted by the United States government!

Several times during the trial, attempts were made to get the men to reveal the location of the silver mine they claimed was nearby, but both of them adamantly refused. One of the men claimed there was enough of the silver ore remaining in the mine to pave every road in the state of Arkansas.

Both men were convicted of counterfeiting and sentenced to several years at Cummins prison farm southeast of Little Rock. The Madison County sheriff visited the men several times during their prison term and tried to persuade them to reveal the location of the silver mine, but still they refused. Attorneys for the two men also tried to learn where the mine was, saying that their sentences might be reduced if they were to provide the information, but they continued to be silent on the subject.

Several Huntsville residents anticipated the release of the two men and their subsequent return to Madison County so that they could tail them to the lost mine. According to relatives of the two, they left immediately for California upon being released from Cummins prison and neither of them ever set foot in Madison County again.

To this day people continue to search for the long-lost silver mine supposedly located near Huntsville, hoping to stumble upon the rich lode the counterfeiters used to make their silver coins. The mine has never been reported found. As far as the residents of Madison County are concerned, it is still lost.

Stone County Silver

Cow Mountain near Timbo in Stone County is reputed to have an ancient silver mine somewhere at the top. Longtime residents of the area believe silver was mined by Indians as recently as the latter part of the last century. Jimmy Driftwood, a three-time Grammy Award winning singer and songwriter and a resident of Timbo, relates this story of the lost silver mine that he heard from his father.

Many years ago, when Stone County was being settled by whites moving into the area, the Native Americans were slowly but most certainly being driven out. One old Indian who frequented the area was not inclined to leave. One day he was chased and caught by a group of farmers who informed him he must vacate the county. The Indian remained steadfast and stoically disregarded their threats. He knew he was too old to fend for himself alone in the wild and rugged portions of the Ozarks that lay to the west, and as he was used to begging food and clothing from the white settlers, he decided he had nothing to lose by resisting.

Presently one of the farmers threw a noose around the old man's neck and dragged him to the nearest oak tree with the intention of hanging him. Seeing the men were determined to kill him, the old man begged for his life and promised his captors that if they spared him he would show them a rich mine atop Cow Mountain. He told the men there was enough silver in the old mine to make them wealthy for the rest of their lives and they could have it if they would just let him live in peace in the area.

His captors agreed to the proposition and on the morning of the next day they followed the old Indian to the mountain. As they approached the ridge, he insisted on blindfolding the men for the remainder of the trip, telling them that it was the Indian way of doing things and that the blindfolds would be removed once they reached the mine. Reluctantly the men agreed.

After a long ride to the top of the ridge along a switchback trail, they arrived at the site of the ancient mine and were allowed to remove their blindfolds. True to his word, the Indian showed them a nearly vertical shaft that extended deep into the mountain. Next to the shaft were several large piles of broken rock that had apparently been dug out of the mine and three smaller piles of loose rock. The Indian pointed to the smaller piles and told the men they would find silver ore mixed in with the rock. The farmers scrambled from their horses and sorted through the small accumulations, filling their pockets and saddlebags with as much of the silver-embedded rock as they could carry.

When they had loaded as much as they could, the Indian reapplied the blindfolds and led the men back down off the mountain.

Two days later the old man disappeared, never to be seen again. It was said that the other Indians who lived nearby had captured and killed him because of the arrangement he had made with the farmers. Carrying his body to the old mine shaft atop Cow Mountain, they threw him in, refilled it, and disguised the entrance so that no one could ever relocate it. Another version of the legend claims that the old Indian learned of the plot to kill him and fled the country.

The farmers made several efforts to find the mine on top of Cow Mountain but never succeeded.

Old Man Napier's Hidden Treasure

During the Civil War, an elderly resident of Mountain Home in Baxter County was reputed to have amassed a substantial fortune that he converted into gold coin. Old man Napier had the reputation of being a cranky tightwad who negotiated the price of everything he purchased. While he made a great deal of money, he had never been known to spend any of it on himself or his family.

Napier always walked everywhere he went, dressed in the same black suit and hat, and carried a cane. He owned and operated several small farms in the region and lived in a well-cared-for two-story house in town.

In the hills outside Mountain Home lived a small band of outlaws who frequented the road into town and preyed on travelers. Robberies were common and the local law enforcement officials seemed ineffective in dealing with the bandits.

One day this group of outlaws rode onto Napier's property in town, barged into his house, and attacked him and his family. Napier, his wife, and his children were bound hand and foot, and the outlaws threatened to kill them all if the old man did not reveal the location of his gold. He refused. The outlaws also tried to get the wife and children to tell, but it was clear they had no idea where the gold had been hidden.

After several minutes the outlaws applied hot irons to Napier's bare flesh, but still he refused to cooperate. The family was dragged out into the front yard and subjected to beatings—all in vain, for Napier refused to talk. As the family and neighbors looked on, the outlaws set fire to the house and barn before mounting up and riding away.

Napier remained under a doctor's care for several weeks while his burns and bruises healed. His family moved into a house on one of his farms, but he remained in town, often visiting the site of his former home and drawing water each day from the brick-walled well between the ruins of the burned-out house and the road.

Within the decade, old man Napier died without ever having revealed the location of his hidden wealth to his wife or children. A man named Bucher purchased the old Napier property and built a fine new house on the site of the one that had been burned down. Bucher chose to ignore Napier's old well and sank a new one closer to the new house, but he kept his milk and butter cool by storing them in the old one.

Stories soon reached Bucher about old man Napier's wealth and the possibility that it was buried somewhere on the property. Bucher dug in promising locations around the house and the old barn but never found anything.

Around 1920, one of old man Napier's granddaughters returned to Mountain Home to visit friends. While there, she decided to ride out to view the old home and property. None of the original buildings was left standing; the only thing remaining that she remembered from her grandfather's home place was the old brick-walled well down by the road.

The granddaughter confirmed the oft-told stories of the huge wealth that was supposedly concealed on the property but said no one in the family ever had any inkling of where the old man hid it. None of the money ever fell into the hands of the relatives, so she presumed it was still hidden—most likely, she said, near the site of the old house or barn.

Several years later, around the time when automobiles were becoming more numerous in Baxter County, a stranger stopped at the old Napier home place. He had been driving across the rough roads of the Ozarks and had sprung a leak in his radiator. He managed to plug the leak, and was now in search of water to refill it. The residents of the old Napier place told the stranger he was welcome to draw as much water as he needed from the old well down near the road.

On the second drawing of the bucket up from the well, the stranger found a gold coin in the bottom of the container. News of the discovery quickly spread around the small community, causing a great deal of excitement among the residents. At last, they believed, Napier's hidden gold had been found.

With the consent of the owners of the property, an attempt was made to enlarge the opening of the well with dynamite so that a man could be lowered to the bottom to retrieve the cache of coins presumed to lie hidden there. On the second effort to widen the shaft, the explosion caused the walls to collapse, filling in the well and perhaps forever burying Napier's hidden gold.

Civil War Treasures

The Lost Payroll

The five Confederate soldiers rode uneasily through the densely wooded area of a remote portion of the Ozark Mountains in northwestern Arkansas. The sergeant, a veteran of several skirmishes, peered into the shadowy foliage all around, ever watchful, ever listening. From time to time he looked back at his detachment—one corporal and three privates—and wished he had been provided with some seasoned soldiers instead of raw recruits. He had been given the responsibility of delivering a large payroll to the Confederate encampment near Prairie Grove, a few miles southwest of Fayetteville. Before he left he was informed by his commander that Union troops were in the area, but as there was a shortage of men, he had to travel without the normal contingent of guards.

As they traveled north along the old military road, the sergeant regarded his four charges. The corporal was barely more than a boy but had proven himself an eager and competent soldier. He had been entrusted with leading the pack horse on which were strapped the bags of gold coin to pay the soldiers at Prairie Grove. Like the sergeant, he was scanning the woods for any sign of the enemy. The three privates were all under seventeen years old and were visibly nervous about the assignment.

The sergeant had turned in his saddle to instruct the corporal to check the fastenings on the payroll bags when a shot rang out from the trees to the left of the detachment. The bullet penetrated the chest of the sergeant, and as he fell from his horse he yelled, "Ambush!"

Several more shots were fired in rapid succession and two of the privates fell from their mounts and were dead before they hit the ground.

The other private was also hit but managed to hang onto his saddle as he spurred his mount up the trail toward Prairie Grove. His wound was bad and he eventually passed out and fell from his horse.

The corporal never had an opportunity to draw his revolver to return fire—he was trying to control his own excited mount as well as maintain a grip on the reins of the pack horse transporting the payroll. Finally, amid the shooting and shouting, the corporal succeeded in turning his horse around and spurring it back in the southerly direction from which the detachment had come. Fearing pursuit, he ran the horses at top speed until it seemed they could go no farther.

Stopping to rest the animals and listen for sounds of pursuit, the corporal spotted a deep crevice in the limestone wall of a cliff rising just off the trail. Quickly he dismounted, retrieved the payroll sacks from the pack horse, and stashed them into the crevice at the base of the cliff. He stuffed rocks, branches, and leaves into the opening to make it look like the rest of the forest floor. He then mounted his horse and, leading the pack horse, returned to his company to report the attack.

When he arrived, he found the camp in a turmoil. Men were rushing around, securing rifles, ammunition, and provisions, and preparing their horses for a forced ride. He sought out the company commander and told him of the attack on the payroll detachment, of escaping the ambuscade, and of concealing the gold along the trail on his return to the camp.

The commander informed the corporal that they would have to attend to the matter of the payroll some other time, because for now they were preparing to go into battle with a force of Union soldiers at Prairie Grove. In a short time, the entire Confederate force was on the march back up the trail.

The Prairie Grove fight was one of the major Civil War battles to take place in Arkansas. The corporal, along with many other Confederate soldiers, was killed during the battle that followed. A few of the troops who were familiar with the story of the corporal and the hidden gold payroll tried to find the cache in later years but without success. The sacks of gold coins are believed to lie concealed in a deep limestone crevice just a few miles south of Prairie Grove along the old military road.

Buried Arms at Cross Hollows

During November 1861, Confederate General Ben McCulloch led an army of 12,000 soldiers into Cross Hollows, a small settlement that had been established some twenty years earlier about ten miles north and slightly east of Fayetteville. Here they were to set up a winter headquarters and serve as an arms and ammunition depot for the war effort.

Several wooden barracks were erected in two long rows that extended about a mile along the valley. Over a period of time, supplies of arms and ammunition were delivered to this location and stored in several frame buildings erected for that purpose. In addition to rifles and pistols, a number of cannons were stored at the Cross Valley location.

One day McCulloch received word that a large contingent of Union troops under the command of General Curtis was approaching the valley. A quick assessment by McCulloch determined he did not have the manpower to withstand an assault by this large Union force, so he gave orders to his men to conceal the arms, destroy the buildings, and abandon the area.

While several men were given the job of burning down all the barracks and supply buildings, the rest hauled rifles, pistols, ammunition, and cannons up an adjacent hill. On a ridge above the valley a long trench was quickly excavated and all the war materials dumped in. The trench was hastily covered, and the men fled the valley.

Several hours later when Curtis and his army arrived at Cross Hollows, all they found were burned buildings and scattered

79

remnants of the Confederate camp. They found no sign of arms and assumed the Confederate soldiers carried everything with them as they retreated toward the south. It never occurred to General Curtis to search the adjacent ridge for the hastily concealed arms.

During the close of the Civil War, many Confederate soldiers who were involved in burying the arms supply on the ridge at Cross Hollows related the tale to others. Several mentioned they would return to the area after the war and retrieve the materials, but none ever did. By the time the war was over, no one seemed to remember exactly where the arms were buried.

Today Cross Hollows is a ghost town. None of the original buildings remain, and there is little to suggest that the site was home to 12,000 Rebel soldiers. Somewhere atop one of the ridges that surround the valley, hundreds of Confederate rifles and pistols along with several cannons still lie buried.

Hidden Treasure on Callahan Mountain

Callahan Mountain is an impressive limestone structure that can be seen just west of Highway 71 between Springdale and Rogers in Benton County.

Many of the people who live near Callahan Mountain are descendants of pioneers who settled in the area before the Civil War, and the following story has been attributed to some of the old-timers who remember hearing it from their parents and grandparents.

During the Civil War, a ragged and depleted company of Confederate soldiers was fleeing a regiment of Union troops. The chase had lasted for nearly two days. As the Rebels' horses were tiring, the men sought a place to hide and defend themselves against the imminent attack.

Spying the gentle slopes of Callahan Mountain, the soldiers climbed it and selected a position that would be defensible against the enemy should they decide to continue the fight.

Before long, the Confederates saw Union troops ascending the slopes behind them. Realizing the battle would soon commence, the contingent of Rebels, about thirty-five in all, elected to hide all their gold, money, watches, and other valuables so that the Yanks would not get them should they prevail.

They quickly dug a hole, placed the valuables into it, refilled it, and rolled a huge stone onto the top. Supposedly it took twenty-one of the soldiers to move the stone into position!

Once the troops engaged, there was an exchange of gunfire that lasted for about two hours. During a lull in the battle the Confederates escaped by descending the western side of Callahan Mountain, intending to return sometime in the future to retrieve the valuables.

Unfortunately, every member of the Rebel company lost his life in the famous Battle of Pea Ridge, which was fought not far from Callahan Mountain just a few days later.

Other Tales of
Treasure in Arkansas

Baxter County Gold

During the early 1940s, a number of men living in the Ozarks earned a meager living hunting and trapping. One such man was named McChord, a congenial fellow who was often seen driving around Baxter County in an old pick-up truck.

Gordon Lambrecht, another Baxter County resident, met McChord. The two struck up a friendship born of their mutual enjoyment of hunting and the outdoors, and spent many hours together exploring remote parts of the Baxter County Ozarks.

After about three months of friendship, McChord asked if Lambrecht would like to accompany him to a secret place he knew of where they could dig for gold. Intrigued, Lambrecht agreed to go along.

The two men rode together in McChord's pick-up truck to the town of Cotter, where they borrowed a small boat from a man who ran a commercial boat dock. They transferred some supplies from the truck to the boat and started upstream. After about a half-hour of travel upriver, McChord turned the small boat into a side stream and followed it for approximately five hundred feet until it got too shallow for them to proceed. McChord banked the craft and unloaded the supplies, and the men walked another six hundred feet up to the top of a hill along a trail that McChord claimed he hacked out himself.

At the top of the hill was an outcrop of rock and evidence of some recent excavation. McChord told Lambrecht that this was his gold mine and instructed him to dig in one certain area.

After an hour of digging, the men returned to the small stream where they panned for ore along the banks. McChord showed Lambrecht how to recognize the small flecks of gold in the bottom of the pan.

Lambrecht was impressed with McChord's knowledge of mining and geology and did as he was instructed. After several hours of labor, the two men had accumulated a small sack of what McChord said was gold ore.

They returned to the boat dock around sundown. Later that evening, McChord cashed in the sack of ore and paid Lambrecht twenty dollars for his labor.

Jesse James in Arkansas

In addition to the extraction of native ore from the rock of the Ozark Mountains, many legends have been passed along concerning such valuables as coins, bills, jewelry, and other items of wealth being secreted in hiding places throughout the range.

Jesse and Frank James and their gang of desperadoes were regular visitors to the Arkansas Ozarks and were known to conceal money from holdups at several different locations. Near the Hickory Creek boat dock on Beaver Lake lies Nelson Hollow Cave, a favorite hiding place for the James gang, where many residents of the area believe some of their loot may be cached.

Another story involving the James gang concerns a bank robbery in Missouri. Frank and Jesse, along with the Younger brothers, took a total of $34,000. They reportedly fled to another favorite hiding place just east of Springdale, Arkansas, and buried the money in a rock crevice at the base of a reddish stone bluff found there.

Mystery Mine In Crawford County

Around the turn of the century a group of men was cutting walnut timber in the vicinity of White Rock Mountain in Crawford County. They spent several days at a time at this endeavor and had established a camp adjacent to Hurricane Creek.

One evening as they were preparing their supper, the timber-cutters were surprised to see a large party of Mexicans ride up. The Mexicans requested permission to camp alongside the creek, and the timber-cutters welcomed them. The group was composed of two elderly men, about twenty-five younger ones, and several women. The caravan consisted of about a dozen light wagons pulled by teams of burros. Most of the younger men rode fine horses.

As the Mexicans set up camp, they unloaded mining tools. Curious, one of the timber-cutters entered the Mexican camp and struck up a conversation with them. In broken English, one of the leaders of the group of Mexicans explained that they had a map and directions to a gold mine in this area that had been worked by their ancestors. They had traveled for many days from far away in Mexico to the Ozarks, intending to find the mine and extract the remainder of the ore.

Over the next few days, several of the younger men struck out into the mountains in search of the mine. One evening they announced they had found it and moved their camp from the creek up into a steep-walled canyon.

For the next several weeks, the timber-cutters heard the sounds of dynamite blasts. Once a day several of the women would drive one of the wagons to the creek to fill water barrels. They told the timber-cutters that the men had found the ancient mine and were excavating the gold.

Eventually, the sounds of blasting were no longer heard. Several of the timber-cutters ventured up into the canyon and discovered that the Mexicans had left. They found the mine shaft easily. A large amount of rock had been removed from it and deposited at the opening of the tunnel. An inspection of the mine revealed no gold whatsoever, and the men decided that the visitors had extracted all that remained and returned to Mexico.

The Lost Snowball Mine

Around 1910 a farmer who lived near Snowball, Arkansas, returned home from a hunting trip with a bucket half full of pure silver ore.

He told his family that he had met some Indian friends in the woods who told him of a silver mine that had been used by the tribe for several generations. They agreed to take the farmer to the mine but insisted on blindfolding him first. When they reached the mine, they showed him a vein of silver about four feet wide running along one wall of the shaft and allowed him to take as much as he could. The farmer cut several large chunks of the pure silver with his hunting knife and placed them in an old bucket he found nearby.

Before they blindfolded him and led him out of the mine and back through the forest, they made him promise never to search for the mine on his own. He agreed.

Many years later he told his son about the trip to the mine, and the son searched for the secret silver mine until he died. The mine has never been found.

MISSOURI

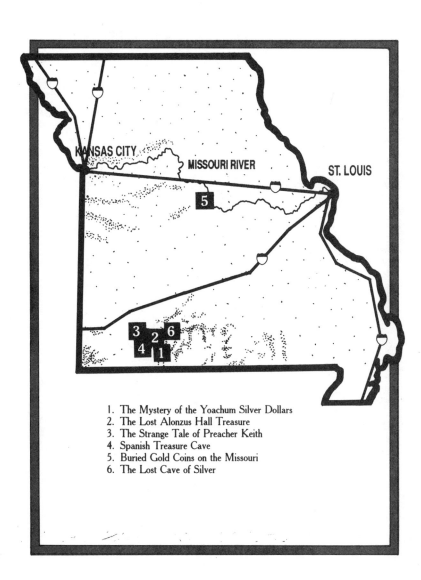

1. The Mystery of the Yoachum Silver Dollars
2. The Lost Alonzus Hall Treasure
3. The Strange Tale of Preacher Keith
4. Spanish Treasure Cave
5. Buried Gold Coins on the Missouri
6. The Lost Cave of Silver

The Mystery of the Yoachum Silver Dollars

One of the most enduring legends of lost and buried trea-
sure ever to come out of the Ozarks concerns the Yoachum
silver dollars. That the silver dollars existed there can be no
doubt—government records clearly substantiate their existence
and several collectors have examples of them. The origin of the
silver and the circumstances involved in the manufacture of the
dollars are still being debated, but the search for the coins and
the mysterious cave from which the silver was allegedly taken is
still going on today.

This story has its beginnings in the year 1541, when Spanish
explorers under the leadership of De Soto penetrated the rugged, isolated valleys of the Ozark Mountains in search of mineral
wealth. Their intention was to locate gold and silver, extract the
ore, smelt it, and ship it back to Spain to fatten the coffers of the
motherland.

A large party of Spaniards explored much of the Ozark Mountain country in southwestern Missouri. The first indications of
ore must have been promising enough to encourage them to
establish a small settlement in the area while the mines were
being developed. They constructed a large log fortress atop
Breadtray Mountain, near the mouth of the James River where
it flows into the White River. The mountain is approximately
three miles northwest of the present town of Lampe, Missouri,
near Table Rock Lake.

The Spaniards were especially delighted with some prospecting near their log fortress. While inspecting an ancient shelter cave long used by Indians, they discovered numerous passageways, one of them containing a thick vein of silver ore. They enslaved several local Indians and put them to work in the cave digging the ore and smelting it into ingots. In no time at all the miners were excavating a tunnel as they followed the vein of silver ore, all the while extracting silver, forming it into eighteen-inch-long ingots, and stacking them against one side of one of the cavern passageways until they could be loaded onto mules and transported to the Mississippi River. From there the ingots were rafted downriver to the Gulf of Mexico, where they were loaded onto a sailing vessel bound for Spain.

The Spaniards treated the Indian laborers cruelly, whipping them if they didn't work at a pace satisfying to the overseers and chaining them at night to prevent their escape. From time to time other Indians were seen observing the fortress and the entrance to the mine from high atop neighboring ridges. Their menacing demeanor made the Spaniards double and triple their nighttime guards.

Hunting parties sent out to find fresh meat often ran into Indians. In some of the confrontations, Spaniards were killed or injured. A few hunting parties sent out never returned.

Increasingly nervous at the growing presence of the hostile Indians, the Spaniards began to discuss the possibility of taking what silver they had accumulated and abandoning the area.

Early one morning a few days later, however, the Indians launched a vicious raid on the fortress and the mine simultaneously. Hundreds of Indians streamed out of the woods and attacked the Spaniards, killing most of them. At the mine all of the overseers were slain and the Indian captives released. A few of the Spaniards escaped, but the silver they had accumulated remained stacked along one wall of the dark cavern.

With the Spaniards gone and the Indians once again dominant in the area, the silver mine remained inactive for over two and a half centuries.

Choctaw legend relates that the cave remained undisturbed until around 1809. During a violent spring thunderstorm, a small hunting party of Choctaws sought shelter in the cave. While waiting out the storm they explored the many passageways that penetrated deep into the mountainside and in this manner discovered the large cache of silver ingots and the old man-made shaft that followed the thick vein of silver ore. They also found several skeletons, no doubt Spanish casualties in the Indian raid over two hundred and fifty years earlier.

The Choctaw traditionally had little use for silver save for the fashioning of ornaments, but contact with white trappers and traders in the area had taught them that they could trade the shiny metal for such supplies as blankets, weapons, and horses. At the entrance of the cave they conducted a two-day ceremony that was intended to drive out the evil spirits they believed resided there.

For many years thereafter, the Choctaw made regular trips to the cave and returned with just enough silver to make jewelry and conduct trade. They carried the silver as far as St. Louis to barter for goods.

One afternoon a Choctaw scout reported a party of Mexicans riding toward the cave along a trail that paralleled the White River. The leader of the Choctaw, accompanied by three armed warriors, rode out to meet the Mexicans and asked the reason for their presence in the Indian homeland.

The leader of the party of Mexicans explained that they were searching for a silver mine that had been excavated over two hundred years earlier, which and they believed was nearby. He unrolled a large sheepskin map replete with Spanish writing and symbols, and the Choctaw chief recognized several prominent area landmarks inscribed on the leather.

After examining the map the chief told the Mexicans that there was no such silver mine in the area and encouraged them to leave.

Fearful that the Mexicans might return and discover the old mine, the chief ordered the entrance to the mine sealed and the area abandoned until he deemed it safe to return. The cave remained closed until a few years later, when other Indians arrived in the valley.

After the War of 1812, the Delaware Indians were relocated into the Ozark Mountains. Originally occupying lands that encompassed parts of Ohio, Indiana, and Illinois, the Delaware were evicted and became involved in a trans-Mississippi migration that landed most of them in the James River area of the Ozarks in southwestern Missouri before 1820. Here they were joined by some Shawnee, Kickapoo, Potawatomi, and Seneca, all likewise evicted from their traditional homelands in the East.

Around this time the Yoachum family also moved into the James River valley and established a farm. The name has been listed in the literature under several different spellings: Yocum, Yokum, Joachim, Yoakum, Yochum, and Yoachum. Most researchers believe the members of the family who settled this area spelled the name "Yoachum."

James Yoachum was born in Kentucky around 1772. A year later his brother, Solomon, was born, and two years after that a third brother arrived, his name being lost to history. While the brothers were still young the family moved to Illinois and tried farming. James had a wanderlust and was not content to work on the family farm. As soon as he turned eighteen, he left the farm and a pregnant wife and decided to seek his fortune trapping in the Ozark Mountains in southwestern Missouri.

James had considerable success in this venture and decided to return to Illinois to get his brothers to accompany him back to the mountains. On arriving at the homestead, he discovered his wife had died in childbirth, leaving him with a son. The boy, named Jacob Levi, was being raised by Solomon and his wife.

James remained in Illinois for several years but still had difficulty adapting to the tedium of farming the flat expanses of the Illinois prairie. Eventually he decided to return to the Ozark Mountains and his trapping enterprise, with the agreement that his two brothers along with their families and Jacob were to join him soon.

On his second trip to the Ozarks, James met and married a Delaware woman named Winona and settled near the confluence of the James and White rivers. Historians claim that the James River was named for James Yoachum, for he developed a very productive farm along the river.

Because of family concerns, the brothers' move to the Ozarks was delayed and they were not able to join James on his farm until 1815. By this time, James Yoachum had planted a large part of the bottoms in corn and squash and had acquired handsome herds of cattle and horses. Most of his neighbors were Delaware Indians, a peaceful people who often brought gifts of food to the new settlers. In return, the Yoachums shared much of their harvest with their new friends, and occasionally presented a gift of a fine horse to a selected member of the tribe.

The Yoachums noticed that the Delaware, as well as members of many of the other tribes living nearby, wore jewelry and ornaments of high-quality silver—long beaded necklaces, arm bands, and hair fixtures. When James inquired about the origin of the silver, the Delaware explained that many years ago an aged Choctaw told them of the existence of a great fortune in silver bars, stacked shoulder-high to a man, in a cave deep in the Ozark forest. A Delaware friend of the Yoachums related the ancient tale of the old cave and the Spanish mine. When James asked if he could see the cave, the Indian told him that it would violate a pact made between the Choctaw and the Delaware tribes never to reveal the location of the silver.

And so it remained for several years, until the federal government initiated an Indian removal process wherein many Native Americans were evicted from their homelands in the Ozarks and resettled on reservations in Indian Territory several miles west in what is now Oklahoma.

As their Indian friends were packing their belongings and loading them onto wagons, the Yoachum brothers arrived to help. They brought gifts for their friends, including blankets, cooking utensils, and horses. In gratitude, several of the Delaware leaders agreed to reveal to the Yoachums the location of the cave from which came the silver. Within days after the departure of the Indians, the Yoachum brothers located the cave. The three men vowed never to reveal the site, and with one exception apparently carried the secret with them to their graves.

When the brothers needed silver from the cave they would ride out from the farm, stay gone for two or three days, and return with several of the ingots that they claimed were taken from a stack of hundreds they found along one wall of the cave. In time they accumulated an impressive pile of silver bars.

As more and more settlers arrived in the Ozarks, and as more and more trading posts became established, the brothers became involved in the commerce of the day. The largest establishment in the area was the James Fork Trading Post, which was managed by a man named William Gilliss. Even though the Yoachums had one of the largest and best farms in the region, they continued to hunt and trap and trade their furs at the James Fork Trading Post for coffee, sugar, flour, and other staples.

The trading post was owned by the business firm of Menard and Valle, operating out of the town of Ste. Genevieve, Missouri. Colonel Pierre Menard, for a long time a good and established friend of the Indian tribes in the Ozarks, watched closely over the trading.

Menard was also very protective of the interests of French trappers in the region. Since the Yoachums were considered outsiders, he told Gilliss to insist that they and others in the area always purchase their supplies with cash. The medium of exchange, thereafter, was no longer to be furs or even gold and silver, but federally issued coin and currency. The Yoachums, though rich in silver, were poor by other standards. They had no money.

In order to remedy this situation, the brothers, under the leadership of James, decided to make their own money. Using simple blacksmith tools, they made some dies, melted down the ingots, rolled the silver out into sheets, and stamped out their own coins. The coins were a bit larger that the ones issued by the government. On one side they bore the inscription "Yoachum" and the date "1822." On the other side was stamped "United States of America" and "1 Dollar."

Over a period of several months thousands of these coins were stamped out and placed into circulation by the brothers. Soon most of the residents of this part of the Ozarks used the coins for any and all kinds of purchases. Gilliss, the manager of the James Fork Trading Post, examined the coins and judged them to be of the purest silver, eagerly accepting them as a legitimate medium of exchange. The Yoachum silver dollars soon became more available in the remote Ozarks than the government-issued money.

This economy worked well for many years. No one outside this remote part of the Ozarks had ever heard of the Yoachum dollars, but residents of the area were happy with the way things were going.

In 1845, however, something occurred to bring the Yoachum dollar to the notice of the federal government. When the lands around the James and White rivers, formerly Indian lands, were opened for purchase by non-Indians, the government sent a surveying crew to establish section lines and county boundaries. During this time the settlers in the area were also notified that they would be required to abide by certain homestead laws relative to securing title to the property on which they lived. Part of the requirement was to pay a filing fee at the government office in Springfield.

Dozens of James River residents intent on paying their filing fee, along with others who wished to purchase some of the newly available Indian lands, arrived at the office in Springfield and tried to pay with the Yoachum silver dollars.

The government agent on duty refused to accept the Yoachum dollars, citing an 1833 regulation that required federally issued coin. He told the settlers that unless they paid in legitimate United States money they could not have official titles to their land.

Enraged, as well as tired from the long journey into Springfield, several of the men pointed loaded guns at the agent and told him that the Yoachum currency meant more to residents in this part of the country than government money and that he had better accept it or suffer the consequences. Fearful for his life, the agent accepted the Yoachum silver dollars and presented each man with a valid certificate to his land.

The agent, being an aggressively dedicated public servant and loyal employee, immediately forwarded the Yoachum dollars along with an explanation of what had occurred to authorities in the nation's capital. Once the coins arrived at Washington, D.C., they were assayed and found to be composed of almost pure silver. In fact, they contained much more silver than the government-issued coin.

Federal authorities did not consider the dollars counterfeit because there was no attempt to duplicate United States government minted coins. Still, they were concerned about the proliferation of non-federal money in the region. They wired the Springfield office and ordered the agent to confiscate Yoachum dollars and to ascertain the location of the silver mine.

Within a few weeks the government agent found his way to James Yoachum's house and announced that he had come to have a look at the silver mine. At gunpoint, Yoachum ordered the agent off his property.

Properly intimidated, the agent left. He returned a week later in the company of eight other federal agents, all well-armed and menacing-looking. This time he explained to James Yoachum the official position of the United States government relative to the locally cast silver dollars and told Yoachum that he was being discouraged from manufacturing and distributing said coins.

Yoachum, considered by many to be a law-abiding and patriotic sort of man, stated he never willfully intended to break any laws. He agreed to stop making the dollars but refused to reveal the location of the silver mine. Discussions continued into the evening with both parties refusing to change their positions. Finally the stalemate was broken when the government agents agreed not to prosecute the Yoachum brothers if they agreed to halt the manufacture and circulation of the coins. The location of the old Spanish mine remained a secret.

Several more years passed, and James Yoachum died. There are two versions of his death. One is that he was taken with a fever and died in his sleep. The other version is that he and his wife, Winona, were killed in a cave-in at the mine on a trip there to retrieve some of the silver. The year was 1848.

After Yoachum's death, the two remaining brothers decided to abandon the Ozarks and go to California. The gold fields were just opening up and the brothers, possessing a strong sense of adventure, were determined to try their luck in a new place. The story has it that before leaving, the brothers gave the dies used in casting the silver dollars to one of the family members who owned a grist mill in the vicinity. Historical records verify that a nephew of James Yoachum owned and operated the largest grist mill in the Ozarks at that time.

The brothers loaded their wagons and left with their families, never to be seen in the Ozarks again. While their fate may never be known, it was told around the James River valley for many years that the brothers, along with their families, died crossing the Rocky Mountains on their way to California. With their death the secret of the location of the old Spanish cave was gone.

Jacob Levi, James Yoachum's son, related a story to his son, Tom, that his father told him after the visit by the government agents. He said that all three brothers went to the cave and sealed it so no one could find it. Jacob often heard his father describe the country around the cave, and he searched for but was never able to find the cave himself. He related this knowledge to Tom, who lived for many years in Galena. Tom, like his father, was never able to find the silver mine.

The legend of the Yoachum dollar has been told and retold many times during the past 160 years and, as with most legends, each retelling is likely embellished. There are, in fact, different versions of the manner in which the brothers located the mine. In addition to the version related above, another claims the Yoachum brothers clandestinely observed local Indians carrying silver bars from the cave. The brothers allegedly killed the Indians who made repeated visits to the cave, concealed the entrance against discovery by others, and altered the trail so that it no longer led to the cave.

Another version of the legend claims that the brothers had no silver mine at all and that the silver used in the Yoachum dollar was simply recast government-issued coin. Before the arrival of the three Yoachum brothers and their families in the James River portion of the Ozarks, the federal government program of relocating the Delaware Indians had long been in place. In addition to the lands assigned, each Indian family was given an annuity of four thousand dollars in silver currency. The Yoachums, greedy for the silver, began making and selling liquor to the Delaware—which was against the law. Not wishing to be caught in possession of the Indian money, they melted it down and recast it using their own handmade dies. To cover their illegal activities, the story goes, the brothers claimed the silver came from a lost Spanish mine they had discovered back in the mountains. The reason the Yoachums were so reluctant to reveal the location of the silver mine, according to researcher Lynn Morrow, was that such a mine never existed.

The above version of the legend suggests that the Yoachum brothers manifested certain outlaw tendencies. This is supported by some documents located in the Missouri Historical Society Archives. A man named John Campbell, who was appointed Indian agent for the James River region, was constantly on the lookout for unscrupulous white settlers who might take advantage of the Delaware. In 1822, Campbell prepared a list of such men. The list includes the name of Solomon Yoachum and suggests he was involved in selling liquor to the Indians. It also suggests that Solomon, James, and the third brother were evicted from the Delaware country for not paying a filing fee on the land.

One version of the Yoachum legend claims that the brothers resettled just outside of the Indian lands near the mouth of the Finley River, where they operated brandy and whiskey stills. It was also said that the Yoachums manufactured the finest peach brandy in the country.

Morrow further contends that the Yoachum brothers knew their silver coin scheme was to be short-lived. When the Delaware were moved out of the Ozark Mountains and relocated farther west in Indian Territory as a result of the James Fork Treaty of 1829, the Yoachums' source of silver left with them. Morrow also noted that after the Indians left the area the Yoachum dollar became scarce.

Whichever version of the legend one chooses to accept, the fact remains that the Yoachum dollar did exist, and that thousands of them were manufactured.

Homer Johnson, a longtime resident of the southwestern Missouri area around Breadtray Mountain, often told a Yoachum silver dollar story that concerned his grandfather, Jefferson Johnson. Jefferson's boyhood friend was Robert Yoachum, a son of Jacob Levi Yoachum, and the two often played together as children. One afternoon the two boys were saddling some horses in the Yoachum barn when Jefferson spied a barrel nearly filled to the top with Yoachum dollars. He estimated there must have been several thousand of the coins in the barrel.

Some of the Yoachum silver dollars have been found: An unidentified man from St. Louis reported in 1974 that, while metal detecting near Branson, he discovered a cache of 236 large silver coins. He described them as being two inches in diameter, roughly cast, and each bearing the inscription "Yoachum" on one side.

Many more of the Yoachum dollars have been recovered and are now in the hands of collectors. It is estimated that many more are yet to be found.

Treasure hunters and coin collectors have long wondered what became of the original dies used for casting the silver dollars. The dies were presumed lost until a remarkable discovery occurred in 1983. On March 11 of that year, J.R. Blunk of Galena was digging near a riverbank on some property near the site of the original Yoachum settlement on the James River. He unearthed a large mass of what appeared to be wax. He broke open the ball of wax and inside found two short sections of iron rod. Scraping wax from the end of one of the rods, Blunk noticed the reverse lettering of the word "Yoachum." On the other rod he was able to discern "1 Dollar."

Excited at his discovery, Blunk spent the next several months researching the Yoachum silver dollar legend and turned up the names of several collectors who owned samples of the original dollars. Through one of the collectors he obtained a Yoachum dollar and, on close examination, realized that it had indeed come from the dies in his possession.

The dies and coin were examined by a professional numismatist named Fred Wineberg who opined that the coins were indeed formed from the dies in Blunk's possession.

But what of the thousands of other Yoachum dollars? What of the barrel full of coins seen in the Yoachum barn by Jefferson Johnson? How many of the coins were hidden away or otherwise disposed of when the government forbade their circulation? How many of the legendary Yoachum dollars are lying forgotten in some moldy old trunk in a dusty attic somewhere deep in the Ozark Mountains?

The Lost
Alonzus Hall Treasure

Alonzus Hall was one of several notorious outlaws who roamed, robbed, and murdered throughout the Ozark Mountains during the Civil War. He has been described as a handsome young man, tall, with deep blue eyes and a charming and disarming smile. A charismatic person, he had little trouble making friends. He was a favorite of the ladies in any settlement he visited, and his confident demeanor and self-possession made it easy for him to assemble a band of followers to help him perpetrate his criminal ways throughout the Ozarks.

Hall was clever and crafty and had a strong sense of adventure and danger. The combination of being high-spirited and mercenary inspired him and his gang to attempt many daring holdups.

One such spate of criminal activity led to Hall's undoing and eventually cost him his life. But before he died, Hall admitted to burying a large fortune in gold coins, a fortune that apparently still lies concealed today in a small cave that is now beneath the waters of Table Rock Lake near the Missouri-Arkansas border.

Alonzus Hall and his gang were well known and feared throughout much of the Ozarks. They primarily ranged from just north of Springfield southward into Arkansas. Because law enforcement was not very sophisticated in this wild land, the bandits raided and pillaged at will, spreading terror throughout the ridges and valleys.

Early in April 1862, the gang was particularly active. The

intrepid Hall led his band of six cutthroats into the settlement of Centralia, Missouri, and at gunpoint robbed the bank of $52,000 in gold coin. Riding from town, the outlaws escaped southward into the hills. The townsfolk were reluctant to pursue them, for they were ill-equipped to chase well-armed and desperate outlaws into the wild, isolated regions where the criminals knew every trail and hiding place.

As the outlaws rode south, they stopped at two small farmsteads. After asking for and receiving food for themselves and grain for their horses, they robbed each of the farmers. At one farm they took $4,000 and at the other $6,000. Then they rode deeper into the secluded mountains.

Captain W.F. McCullough (sometimes spelled *McCulla)* was in command of a company of Union soldiers temporarily encamped near the Frisco Railroad tracks about twenty-five miles west of Springfield when he received word of the bank robbery at Centralia. McCullough had been following the Hall gang for several months, and now was ordered to search for them and to try to capture them at any cost.

The day after the bank robbery, McCullough received word that the outlaws had been seen traveling south along the old Wilderness Road and were last spotted in Greene County. He immediately ordered his men to pursue the bandits. The soldiers rode twelve hours straight without a break, hoping to overtake them within the next day or two. The outlaw trail led the soldiers through Greene County, into Christian County, and finally into Stone County and to the White River.

On the evening of the second day, one of the army scouts reported to McCullough that he had spotted the outlaws camped under a ledge near the bank of the White River about a mile away. At the same time, one of the outlaws who had been posted as a lookout had spotted the approaching soldiers and immediately alerted the others.

On receiving the news of the approaching army, Hall and another of the outlaws gathered up the gold coins and other money and carried it to a nearby cave. They divided the loot into four equal piles, stuffed each into a buckskin bag, and hastily scraped out a shallow trench in the floor of the cave into which they placed the sacks. They covered the site with rocks and debris to conceal any traces of digging. By now Hall and his companion could hear gunshots coming from the campsite and knew that the soldiers had engaged his men in a battle. Hall and his companion raced toward the campground to join in the fight.

McCullough had launched a vicious attack on the desperadoes, who were heavily outnumbered and out-armed. The fighting was brief, lasting only about five minutes. By the time it was over, three of the Union troops and six of the outlaws were killed. Alonzus Hall had been shot through the stomach and was in poor shape when the soldiers found him.

Hall was bandaged, loaded into a wagon, and transported to a temporary bivouac area along the White River near present-day Reeds Spring. He suffered terribly throughout the night and the next day was taken to the Union Army General Hospital at Springfield.

The attending surgeon summoned to examine Hall's wound was Dr. Boucher (sometimes spelled *Bushay* and *Busha*). After looking at Hall's wound, Boucher deduced that a musket ball had penetrated his lower intestines, doing irreparable damage. He predicted Hall would not live for more than a day or two.

Several hours later Hall regained consciousness and Boucher informed him of his condition. Hall appeared silent and moody but resigned to his fate.

The next morning, however, he called Boucher to his bedside and asked if he could make a confession. As the surgeon was the ranking officer in the camp at the time, he agreed to take Hall's statement. Securing a hospital journal, he scribbled copious notes as the outlaw leader related the story of the recent robbery spree.

Hall told Boucher all that had transpired from the time of the Centralia Bank holdup until the attack by the Union soldiers at the campground on the White River. He said that the $62,000 was buried in a cave near the old ferryboat crossing where the Wilderness Road met the White River. He also asked Boucher to make certain the money he took from the farmers was returned to them.

Boucher took explicit notes of the confession, filling several pages of the journal. The next morning when he went to visit Hall, he found the patient had died.

Boucher was confused about what to do with Hall's information. His military training told him he should immediately file it with his superiors, but the potential wealth lying buried in a shallow cave less than a day's ride from the camp tempted him greatly. With dreams of riches awaiting him, Boucher hid the journal, expecting someday soon to be able to travel to the intersection of the Wilderness Road and the White River to retrieve the gold.

All too soon, however, the surgeon was transferred to a more active military post in the East. He left the journal hidden among some files in the hospital at Springfield, hoping to return for it.

There is no record that Boucher ever returned to Springfield. Hospital personnel discovered the journal a few years later.

By the turn of the century several people had read the notes in his journal. The descriptions of the robbery and subsequent flight of the outlaws through the Ozark Mountains were quite vivid, as were the accounts of the encounter with the Union soldiers and burying the $62,000 in gold coin and other money in the shallow cave.

The journal contained a thorough description of the cave in which the gold had been buried. Hall had said the cave was not very far from the overhanging ledge where they encountered the soldiers, because once they buried the loot it was only a very few minutes until the outlaw leader and his companion returned to the fray. The cave was described as being slightly illuminated as a result of sunshine beaming through a narrow crack in the limestone roof. The men buried the loot in the cave floor at the approximate center of the shaft of light.

It is an easy task to locate the point at which the old Wilderness Road intersects with the White River—it is quite apparent on the many maps of the region. It would also seem easy to locate the overhanging ledge under which the outlaws camped, as well as any small caves in the area. An overriding problem in the search for Hall's treasure, though, is that the rising waters of Table Rock Lake are believed to have completely submerged this site.

Near where the loot is thought to have been buried, the Kimberling (sometimes spelled *Kimberly)* Bridge has been built. Some say the construction of the bridge may have obliterated any traces of the overhang and the cave. Others claim that the site is intact but lies under several feet of lake water.

There is no evidence that the gold and money buried by Alonzus Hall were ever recovered. The consensus of most researchers of this event in Ozark history is that the treasure still lies in a shallow excavation in a small cave somewhere beneath the waters of Table Rock Lake.

The Strange Tale of Preacher Keith

One of the most bizarre tales ever to come out of the Ozarks involves an itinerant preacher and the strange way he hid his wealth. Residents of the Ozark Mountains in southwestern Missouri still talk about Preacher Keith. A few of his relatives who still live in the region maintain that the legends of this eccentric man and his lost fortune in gold are all true.

W.M. Keith arrived in the Missouri Ozarks around 1830. It is believed that he came from the Red River Valley area of Oklahoma, near where that great and muddy river was crossed by the Chisholm Trail. No one has an explanation for why he left Oklahoma and traveled east to the Ozarks. He arrived carrying only the clothes on his back and a well-worn Bible.

Shortly after Keith came to Missouri, he constructed a rude cabin near Reeds Spring. From the moment of his arrival, his neighbors regarded him as a bit odd. A tall and gangly man of Lincolnesque stature and profile, Keith had a habit of talking aloud to himself as he walked for miles up and down the area roads from dawn until dusk with no apparent destination in mind.

He survived well by living off the land, hunting, trapping, and performing seasonal jobs for area farmers. In spite of his odd manner, he was regarded as a competent worker and was generally well-liked.

After Keith had been in the area for several months, he proclaimed himself a preacher and filled his Sundays with visiting outlying areas and holding church services for any and all who would come to hear him. He loudly interpreted the Bible to the many hill folk who came to listen, conducting services in barns or under the shade of a convenient tree.

Soon he met and married a young girl whose name was Lee. Keith and his bride moved into the cabin near Reeds Spring and began to raise what ultimately became a large family.

Keith provided well for his family. In addition to the few coins passed on to him for his preaching and what he made from hunting and trapping, he planted the hillside near his cabin in corn. As his family grew he added extra rooms to the rustic cabin. He seemed to be a good husband and father.

In 1849, Preacher Keith heard about the discovery of gold in California. The lure of wealth waiting to be found in that faraway land was irresistible to him and, bidding his wife and children goodbye, he set out for the Golden State with the hope of striking it rich. And strike it rich he did.

Keith had great success in the California gold fields. After a year of panning the clear cold streams of the Sierra Nevada Mountains, he had accumulated a relatively large fortune. He converted his ore into gold coins, purchased passage on a steamer, sailed around the horn of South America, and eventually landed in New Orleans. There he bought two mules, onto which he loaded several leather sacks filled with his gold coins. He and the mules walked the entire distance from New Orleans back to the Ozark Mountains, where his family held a joyous reunion.

News of the preacher's fortune soon spread throughout this part of the Ozarks, and Keith became visibly annoyed that so many of his neighbors were aware of his wealth. He grew suspicious of all who chanced by his cabin and assumed that everyone was intent on taking his gold away from him. He threatened many visitors with his rifle and was known to stay awake nights guarding his property.

After several weeks of worrying about the security of his fortune, Keith loaded the gold onto the mules and carried it out into the woods beyond the cabin. Far from the prying eyes of his neighbors and family, he hid it in a location that remains secret to this day.

For reasons he never explained, Keith refused to reveal to members of his family the location of his wealth. His relatives claim he undertook and completed the task of hiding the gold in no longer than one hour, so it is assumed the fortune was stashed close to the old log cabin. Some believe the sacks of gold coins were secreted in one of the many limestone caves in the area.

Others who have researched the legend of Preacher Keith believe the eccentric fellow buried the gold somewhere near his orchard of apple, peach, and cherry trees, a source of pride for him. He spent many long hours pruning the trees and tending to the grove, which was a short distance from the cabin just beyond the immediate woods. Some say that when Keith needed a little cash, he would disappear into the woods in the direction of his orchard and reappear a few minutes later carrying a single twenty-dollar gold piece. He always laughingly informed people that the gold coins grew on the trees in his orchard.

Another strange twist to the Preacher Keith legend is the belief that he walled up the front of one of the caves in a nearby mountain and stashed his gold within.

From time to time Keith was observed hauling slabs of rock back into the woods some distance from the cabin. He would be gone for several hours, sometimes shooing away any who came near. When he returned to his cabin at the end of the day he had mortar splashed across the front of his overalls. Occasionally he would mention a "room" he was building in which he was going to hide his gold where no one could ever find it.

Keith also told of fashioning a large wooden door for the rock enclosure. He claimed the door was eight feet tall and four feet wide and made of heavy oak timbers that he cut and planed himself. Supposedly the huge door was fastened shut with a stout lock.

As if this were not strange enough, rumor also circulated that Keith had built a casket inside the small room of the walled-up cave! He claimed to his family one day that he had constructed a long casket from hand-riven pine boards. He said that when he was ready to die he would go to the walled-up room, lock the door, and lie in the casket surrounded by his wealth to wait for his Maker's call.

Preacher Keith visited his private hoard at least once a week for many years. During all that time his family had no inkling of the location of the cave or his treasure and, in spite of constant questioning, he refused to tell them.

As he grew older his behavior became more erratic and unpredictable. Fewer and fewer people showed up for his Sunday services, and most of the area residents believed the old man was touched.

None of this bothered Keith. He continued with his hunting and trapping and growing corn on the bare soil of the Ozark hillsides, providing for his family, and, despite the diminishing attendance at his services, preaching his Sunday sermons.

One morning Preacher Keith announced to his family that he was going hunting. He left the cabin after breakfast, walked out into the woods carrying his rifle, and was never again seen alive.

People in Reeds Spring just presumed Preacher Keith went to his mysterious cave and laid himself down to eternal rest in his homemade casket, surrounded by the twenty-dollar gold pieces he had hoarded so effectively for so long. They combed the woods near his cabin for several weeks after his disappearance but found neither the man nor the cave. Several people focused their search around the orchard, still believing that the wealth was concealed nearby, but they had no luck. Eventually the search was halted.

About two months after the disappearance of Preacher Keith, a local man was out hunting one evening when he discovered a badly decomposed corpse in an abandoned orchard in a hollow about four miles south of the Reeds Spring settlement. The body was seated on the ground and leaning up against the bole of a cherry tree. A rifle lay across its lap.

The hunter went for help and returned with three companions. They examined the body thoroughly but could find no wounds. Figuring the man must have died from a heart attack, they buried the body beneath the tree where it was found.

The men noticed that several large holes had been dug throughout most of the orchard, as though someone had been searching for something—what, they could not determine.

When word of the dead man reached Reeds Spring, several members of the Keith family went to see the hunter who had made the grisly discovery. He described the clothing and boots worn by the corpse and produced the rifle that was with it. The family agreed that the dead man must have been W.M. Keith.

What actually happened to Preacher Keith will probably never be known. Some believe that the old abandoned orchard in which he was found held the secret to his gold and that his cryptic comments about his gold growing on trees referred not to the orchard behind his cabin but to the one in which his body was discovered. The many holes in the abandoned orchard remain a mystery.

To this date the walled-up cave in which the eccentric old preacher was supposed to have hidden his gold has never been discovered.

And the empty casket must still lie in the dark room amidst the piles of gold coins, forever waiting for the owner who will never return.

Spanish Treasure Cave

Few legendary buried treasure locations in the Ozarks have received more attention than a mysterious cave about four miles north of Reeds Spring in Stone County.

There is little doubt among researchers that a fabulous wealth in gold and silver lies concealed deep within this cavern. However, a number of cave-ins and excavation attempts have combined to rearrange the interior passageways and chambers so that it now bears little resemblance to the site the Spaniards chose in the sixteenth century for caching a great fortune in gold and silver ingots.

In recent years a portion of the cave was made available for tourists who would make the short drive to the entrance from nearby Highway 65. The cave differs little from the many other limestone caves in the region, but a hundred years ago it was the center of one of the most intensive treasure hunts ever witnessed in the Ozarks.

The story begins sometime in 1888, though the exact date is uncertain. An old man, most often described as a Spaniard, appeared one day in the settlement of Joplin looking for work. He was hired to mop out one of the local taverns on a nightly basis, but had not been employed long when he came down with a serious illness, probably tuberculosis. Two men, Joplin residents and patrons of the tavern in which the old Spaniard was employed, took pity on the poor sick man, brought him to their room at a nearby hotel, and tended to his ailment. When he got progressively worse, a physician was summoned. After examining the Spaniard the doctor proclaimed he was dying and had very little time left.

After the doctor left the old man summoned his two new friends to his bedside. He weakly waved an arm toward his small pile of modest belongings in the corner of the room and told the two men he wanted them to have his money and possessions in gratitude for their care. The two friends sat up the entire night with the old man, but by dawn he was dead.

Later that day when the men examined the old Spaniard's belongings they found only a few coins, almost enough to provide for a decent burial. The few garments he owned were little more than rags and the men elected to throw them away. As they gathered up the old clothes, a rolled parchment fell from the inside of an old worn coat. Examining it, the two men discovered it to be a map with legends and notations in Spanish. Applying what little Spanish they knew, they interpreted a most amazing story from the old parchment map.

Sometime during the sixteenth century, a group of Spanish soldiers and laborers under the command of one of Hernando De Soto's officers were transporting twenty mule-loads of gold and silver ingots through the Ozarks. The ore had been taken from mines far to the southwest in Texas and was being transported to the Mississippi River, where it was to be loaded onto flatboats, rafted to the Gulf of Mexico, and shipped to Spain. As the Spaniards wound their way through the Ozarks with the pack train in tow, they searched for signs of precious ore.

During an extended encampment in what is now southwestern Missouri, the Spaniards discovered a vein of silver in a cave, and the leader of the group gave orders to begin mining immediately. A crude log fort was constructed as protection against the coming winter and marauding Indians. The mining proceeded smoothly, but Indian attacks occurred with increasing frequency. Eventually the Spaniards decided to hide their gold and quit the area until it seemed safe to return.

After interpreting the old treasure map, the two friends decided that the old Spaniard had come into the Ozarks in search of the long-lost treasure cache and mine but apparently was never able to locate it.

Several weeks after the Spaniard's burial, the two men undertook a search for the cave described on the map. According to the description, the cave was supposed to be in a remote part of Stone County. The map indicated the search was to begin near three large trees arranged in a triangle. Each of the trees had strange crescent-shaped markings blazed onto the trunk. The markings pointed to the site of the fort constructed by the Spanish soldiers, which was supposed to be at the base of an overhanging bluff. Nearby, along the base of the same bluff, was the entrance to the treasure cave.

The map indicated the cave entrance was covered and disguised to look exactly like the rest of the bluff. To gain entrance to the cave a barrier had to be removed, exposing a low narrow opening. Once inside, however, the cave was large enough for a tall person to stand. The passageway extended deep into the bluff for over half a mile to where the ingots were stacked. As one explored the passageways, one would pass through thirteen large chambers, each containing impressive cavern formations. At the fourteenth and final chamber, one would find the cache of gold and silver hidden there by the Spaniards in 1522.

The two men searched for the three large trees arranged in a triangle but were never able to locate them. For two years they combed the area when time permitted, always hoping to discover some telltale sign that would lead them to the treasure cave. Finally, after investing two years and a great deal of money in the fruitless search, they gave up and declared the whole episode a hoax. They turned the map over to a Webb City newspaper, which printed it in 1890.

A few months later, one of these newspapers came into the possession of a Stone County resident named J.J. Mease. Mease was no stranger to gold; he had hoped to strike it rich in the California Gold Rush of 1849 but finally came away with nothing. Discouraged, he returned to his Ozark Mountain homeland, but his dream of someday discovering gold remained very much alive.

Mease prospected for gold and silver throughout Stone County for a number of years. Following promising leads, he had opened several shafts in the hope of locating silver, but thus far it had eluded him.

Mease was as familiar with the terrain in Stone County as anyone, and when he examined the description of the old Spanish treasure cave in the newspaper, he was convinced he knew the location. He contacted a friend named H.R. Brewer and together they systematically searched for the cave.

One day in the summer of 1894, Mease and Brewer discovered the three large trees with barely discernible crescent-shaped markings on the trunks. Following the signs on the trees, the two men came to a high, overhanging limestone bluff. Near one end of the deeply recessed base of the bluff they found the rotted remains of several large logs and deduced they must have been part of the Spanish fort described on the map. The men observed that the fort had been situated in an ideal site—the overhanging bluff afforded protection from the weather and the position was quite defensible against the potential attack of hostile Indians. Several springs gushing clear cool water were found nearby.

But further examination of the bluff from one end to the other revealed no evidence of a cave! Several times Mease and Brewer searched back and forth along the rock wall, each time coming away perplexed. According to the map and the evidence this had to be the correct site, but they could find nothing.

Mease and Brewer enlisted the help of several neighbors, and soon nearly a dozen men were combing the area in search of some sign of a cavern opening. One afternoon, one of the men, H.O. Bruffet, was idly digging in the soil along the face of the bluff that had been examined at least a dozen times previously. Approximately a foot below the surface Bruffet unearthed a copper bowl. The other searchers were summoned, and together they examined the find. After cleaning most of the dirt from the vessel, Mease pointed to several Spanish symbols engraved into it. On a hunch the men began digging into the ground where the bowl had been discovered. After removing approximately three feet of earth they made an astounding discovery. There, under the layer of dirt that had covered it for centuries, was a large flat stone slab standing vertically against the base of the bluff. On its face were carved several symbols that matched many of the symbols on the old parchment map. All this time it had never occurred to the men that the cave's entrance lay below the very soil they walked over. The level of the ground at the base of the bluff had been raised to conceal the entrance!

With considerable effort the men hammered the large stone into smaller pieces and removed it. Behind it was a low, narrow opening into a cave. Within the small entrance were several piles of ashes and charcoal suggesting human use or occupation some time in the past.

Just beyond the ashes, the floor of the cave dropped abruptly for a dozen feet before it leveled out again. Three men were lowered by rope to the bottom of the dangerous drop, where they discovered three skeletons. Among the bones were found odd pieces of metal that the men decided were parts of Spanish armor.

Also lying among the bones and artifacts was an ancient mold made of porcelain that was used to form ingots. The mold was six inches deep and approximately two and a half feet long. The inside of the mold was coated with a thin film of silver.

Along one side of the cavern wall at the bottom of the drop were several more inscriptions similar to the ones found on the stone slab that covered the opening.

Convinced that this was indeed the legendary cave that held the long-hidden Spanish treasure, the men agreed to form a company to remove the hoard and split the wealth equally. One of the men, C.C. Bush, volunteered to journey to Galena, the nearest large settlement, to obtain a formal deed to the land on which the cave was located. It turned out that the land was owned by the Frisco Railway, which agreed to sell it to the group for three dollars an acre. The men all contributed equally and purchased several acres of the surrounding land.

Several days later as the group began clearing away the soil and enlarging the opening to the cave, a young man appeared on the scene making inquiries about the digging. He was tall and well-dressed in the manner of an attorney. His skin was olive-colored and he spoke with a distinct Spanish accent. After querying area residents about the excavation in process, he appeared at the scene of the digging.

When introductions had been made, the newcomer came quickly to the point of his visit and made an offer of one thousand dollars for the deed to the land on which the excavation was taking place.

The men refused to sell. They had believed they were indeed on the threshold of finding and retrieving the long-lost Spanish fortune, and the appearance of this young Spaniard offering them a large amount of money convinced them that something of value was to be found inside the cave.

A few days elapsed since the Spaniard first appeared, and during that time Mease and Brewer became good friends with him and learned his reason for wanting to purchase the property.

The Spaniard had in his possession an ancient map similar to the one that had been found many years earlier in the belongings of the dead man at Joplin. This map resembled the one Mease had seen in the Webb City newspaper—it told of the twenty mule-loads of gold and silver, the fourteen chambers to be found inside the cave, and the existence of a thick vein of silver in the fourteenth chamber, a vein of almost pure ore that was mined and smelted by De Soto's men nearly four hundred years before.

The young Spaniard continued to make offers to the men, but all were refused. He left the area quietly and was never seen there again.

Once the opening of the cave had been enlarged and the hazard of the sudden drop overcome, the group entered the cave armed with torches, digging tools, and abundant enthusiasm.

Almost immediately they encountered problems. The floor of the cave was extremely difficult to traverse. Large chunks of rock had fallen from the fractured roof and blocked passage throughout. Water dripped continuously from the ceiling, making the footing slippery. The way through the cave was crooked and replete with sudden drops and rises, and it was only with great difficulty that the men were able to make any progress at all.

The first day of searching the cave took nearly fourteen hours and saw the discovery of only the first three of the large chambers referred to on the maps. One of the men suffered a broken leg and had to be carried out, a task that required almost two days.

On the next attempt to locate the treasure cache, the men carried a large supply of torches and candles as well as provisions to last for forty-eight hours. Their enthusiasm had remained undiminished, but this time they proceeded with greater caution, worrying and wondering what obstacles they might next confront.

On and on they pushed—crawling, walking, climbing, and sliding—for many hours. Finally they passed the thirteenth chamber. Spurred on by the anticipation of finding great wealth at the next turn in the dark passageway, they crawled forward only to encounter their greatest disappointment. When they arrived at what was to have been the fourteenth chamber they discovered it had been effectively sealed by a huge cave-in, with thousands of tons of rock and debris blocking the entrance.

Armed with only picks and shovels, the men began digging into the rubble, but it soon became obvious that they were unequal to the task. The mass of rock that stood between them and the treasure would take months, probably years, to remove by hand.

Discouraged, the men slowly made their way back to the surface to report their disappointment.

After many discussions, the company of men decided that whatever treasure might lie hidden deep within the inaccessible fourteenth chamber inside the mountain was not worth the effort it would take to excavate. The project was abandoned and the company dissolved, and all returned to their businesses, farms, and families.

The dream of finding the hidden wealth did not die in one of the men, however. Frank Mease, the son of J.J. Mease, was only a young boy at the time of the excavation. Frank Mease participated in the digging as enthusiastically as any of the men, doing far more than his fair share of work. He, more than any of the others, was terribly disappointed when it was announced the project was to be abandoned.

Like his father so many years before, Frank Mease nurtured a dream of wealth. As he grew to manhood he continued to nourish his dream—a dream that someday he would be the one to break into that mysterious fourteenth chamber and retrieve the ancient Spanish fortune.

Frank Mease decided to approach the problem of finding the treasure differently. He decided the task of removing the tons of rock debris could be made simpler if lights and power were available to men digging deep below the surface. Heretofore, tallow candles and grass torches had supplied the only light, and Mease believed there was a better way.

He observed that a swiftly flowing stream paralleled the main passageway through the cave. In order to use the energy of the flowing water, he constructed a flume that directed the stream to an area where he constructed a waterwheel turned by the flowing water. The wheel activated a generator that provided electricity for workers in the cave.

Once Mease had strung electric lights throughout most of the passageways and up to the fourteenth chamber, he examined the possibilities of directing some of the flowing water so that it would remove and carry away much of the rock and debris blocking the entrance to the treasure chamber.

As he was making arrangements to begin construction of his labor-saving idea, bad fortune befell the inventive Mease. A huge portion of the cavern roof gave way, and thousands of tons of weakened and crumbling limestone rock crashed to the floor, making passage beyond the third chamber impossible.

With the sudden cave-in, months of planning and labor vanished. After examining the disaster, Mease decided it would be impossible to penetrate the new obstacle.

Being an enterprising man, however, he attempted to make

the best of the unfortunate situation. Advertising the cave as the "Lost Spanish Treasure Cave," he graded a good road from nearby Highway 65 and charged tourists a small admission to visit the cave entrance, where he related the story of the lost treasure. As he profited from this enterprise, he built a gas station and a hotel at the intersection of the dirt road and the highway.

Given the existing research, the available evidence, and the huge investment of time and energy of many men, there seems to be little doubt that a great fortune in Spanish gold and silver does exist deep inside the limestone bluff in Stone County. Several experts on caverns in the Missouri Ozarks claim the Spanish treasure cave is most likely part of an extensive cavern system that runs for several miles deep below the surface. For many years people have searched for a passageway from one of the other caves in this system that might connect with the blocked fourteenth chamber of the Spanish treasure cave. A group of engineers has discussed sinking a vertical shaft from some point on the top of the bluff in an effort to enter the treasure chamber, but the exact below-ground position cannot be determined.

Others have maintained that when the Spaniards hid the treasure deep in the cave they placed a curse on it. The curse provided for disaster to befall any who would attempt to retrieve the great treasure except for the rightful heirs. If one believes in such curses, one must assume this one is still effective.

Buried Gold Coins
on the Missouri

The northern limits of the Ozark Mountains gradually change from the rugged dissected uplands of the interior. Here, near the Missouri River, one does not see the sharp features of the high ridges and deep valleys so often associated with the Ozarks, but rather a series of smoother, undulating hills broken here and there by level patches of prairie and floodplain.

Prosperous farms are found along the level plains adjacent to the Missouri River, with healthy crops growing from the rich dark alluvial soils. In places, ceaseless erosion by the river has exposed bluffs of the more resistant limestone rock of the Ozarks, bluffs that may extend to the river itself. Near one of these bluffs, in 1802, four French traders buried a copper kettle filled with gold coins.

At the beginning of the nineteenth century, St. Louis was the last settlement encountered by trappers, traders, adventurers, and any who would dare to brave the uncharted wilderness that lay to the west. To venture up the relatively unknown Missouri River and its tributaries to the faraway trading posts and beaver streams of Rocky Mountain wilderness was indeed a bold undertaking, for the dangers were many.

Trading posts had been established at the confluences of the Kaw, Republican, Platte, and other rivers, and it was to these sites that the trappers brought their beaver pelts each year to trade for supplies and equipment or to sell for gold.

Several times a year the Missouri River hosted relatively

heavy boat traffic as a result of the loads of furs being floated to St. Louis and the bundles of trade goods and chests of gold being carried to the trading posts upriver.

Some time during the second week of October 1802, a small wooden craft plied up the Missouri, rowed by four Frenchmen employed by a St. Louis-based fur trading company. They were transporting gold coins to trading posts far upriver for use in purchasing prime beaver pelts. In the center of the wooden craft sat a copper kettle filled to the top with gold coins of French origin. In addition to the gold there were several bundles of trade goods, but the primary responsibility of the Frenchmen was to protect the gold shipment—with their lives if necessary.

Rowing upstream on the Missouri River was no easy task, and the party of Frenchmen had not been on their journey long when they began to wish for it to end. They were eager to deliver the gold and the trade goods and be well on their way back to St. Louis before the first winter storms struck the area.

For several days the men rowed, slowly yet unceasingly forging their way against the strong current. Once leaving St. Louis, they were constantly on guard against hostile Indians known to frequent the region. At night they made camp on the riverbanks and posted a lookout. When they ventured inland to hunt for fresh meat, they always divided, one pair hunting while the other remained close to the boat and guarded the gold.

The Frenchmen had not seen a single Indian the entire time they had been on the river. They soon grew complacent and, while previously they constantly scanned the riverbanks with apprehension, they were now content to take turns napping.

Early in the evening of the fifth day of their journey, the men were rowing along and searching the riverbank for a suitable place to camp. They had passed several miles of low bluffs ranging along the south bank, looking for one set slightly back from the water and recessed enough to protect them from the weather.

As they examined the bluffs, dozens of screaming Indians came charging out of the willow break on the opposite shore. As the Frenchmen looked on in horror, the howling mob began

121

firing arrows at them and launching canoes into the river.

Grabbing oars, the four Frenchmen bent their backs to the rowing until the boat fairly skimmed across the surface of the water. In spite of their efforts, however, the small, light canoes of the Indians were gaining on them rapidly.

When it became obvious that the greatly outnumbered Frenchmen would soon be overtaken, they steered their boat to the south bank, deciding it would be easier to defend themselves on solid ground than in a boat on the river.

Landing, the men grabbed their firearms and some belongings and raced about sixty yards to the shelter of a nearby bluff. Two of the Frenchmen quickly returned to the boat, lifted the heavy kettle of coins, and wrestled it to the sanctuary of the bluff.

The sun was beginning to set just as the last two men reached the shelter. Hurriedly, they stacked rocks and tree limbs into an improvised fortress as they prepared for an attack from their pursuers.

The Indians beached their canoes and advanced. As they approached the shelter, a shot rang out from under the bluff and a musket ball penetrated the skull of one of the nearest Indians, dropping him immediately and causing the others to scatter for cover.

During the night the Frenchmen could observe the Indians moving about in the dark, establishing themselves in a semi-circle enclosing the bluff, effectively cutting off any escape route to the boat. The Indians made small camps of two to three men each and built fires to warm them from the chill of the autumn darkness. Throughout the night the four frightened Frenchmen watched the Indian campfires and dreaded the approaching dawn.

Daybreak was accompanied by the sudden arrival of a premature winter storm. A thick, heavy snow fell, reducing visibility to only a few feet, and accumulated to a depth of several inches within two hours. The storm appeared to inhibit the Indians' desire to launch an attack and they remained close to their fires. Once in a while one of them would shoot an arrow into the makeshift fortress under the bluff.

The Frenchmen made themselves as comfortable as possible under the adverse circumstances, but they were gradually running low on firewood and food. One of the men suffered severe frostbite and lay in agony near the small fire.

Another man who ventured forth to get food from the boat was attacked not far from the fortress and was forced to retreat to the shelter.

For four days the Frenchmen remained trapped. During that time the man suffering frostbite died and was buried during the dark of night a short distance from the bluff. The three remaining Frenchmen decided their only chance for survival was to make a break for the boat and try to return to St. Louis.

They realized they would never be able to carry the heavy gold-filled copper kettle while they made their escape, so just after sundown of the fourth day, they carried it some distance from the fortress and buried it, hoping to return for it in the future. After waiting for several hours in the hope that most of the Indians would be sleeping, the three stole quietly into the night toward the river.

Halfway to the boat they were discovered by Indian scouts. The race was on. Firing their single-shot muskets into the group of pursuers, the Frenchmen managed to kill two of the Indians during their flight. Unfortunately, however, only one of the traders made it to the boat.

In pain from severe arrow wounds, the surviving Frenchman launched the boat into the river and, lying in the bottom of the craft, let the current carry him downstream toward St. Louis. For unknown reasons the Indians did not take up pursuit.

Bleeding profusely and lapsing in and out of consciousness, the lone Frenchman floated easily down the river it had taken so much effort to travel only a few days earlier. Somehow he reached St. Louis. Delirious and near death, he was taken from the boat and carried to a physician. The medical man treated the poor trader's arrow wounds and frostbite, but his limbs were so badly frozen that they had to be amputated.

Several days later when the Frenchman regained consciousness, he related the story of the Indian attack, the loss of his comrades, the burying of the gold, and the harrowing escape. He provided a representative of the French fur trading company with a detailed description of the bluff under which the men had taken shelter and told them precisely where the gold was hidden. The fur trading company decided to send a party of men in the spring to retrieve it.

When spring came, however, no such search party was to be sent out because of the recurring news that the Indians of the region were in a hostile mood and had killed several traders trying to pass through the territory.

The following year the trading company organized a group of French trappers to journey to the bluff and retrieve the gold. This group was beset with bad luck, and after several days of travel they all suffered an attack of dysentery and had to return to St. Louis. The fur trading company had other business to attend to, and soon the matter of the buried copper kettle filled with gold coins was forgotten.

In 1835, a large group of French trappers undertook a journey up the Missouri River from St. Louis toward the rich trapping grounds of the Rockies. Five boats in all carried the members of this well-armed party. The sight of these seasoned mountain men must have discouraged Indian attacks, for none of the hostiles was seen.

Several men in this party could recall the story of the buried coins and were determined to search for them. But in the vicinity of the bluff, they encountered a surprise. The ever-shifting channel of the Missouri River had moved. A great flood had caused the river to jump its banks and cut a new channel about a quarter of a mile north of the old one. Still, the men believed that with a little luck they could find the gold. They established a camp along the river and spent several weeks searching the area but were never able to locate the buried wealth.

Years passed, and the once-fertile beaver streams of the Rocky Mountains were being trapped out. The shrinking supply, coupled with the reduced demand for the belly fur of the beaver for hats, signaled the end for trappers and traders in this part of the country. Human traffic up and down the Missouri River diminished to almost nothing. Not until after the Civil War did settlers began swarming westward again, across the Mississippi River and toward the Rocky Mountains and the Pacific coast.

Several newcomers discovered the rich alluvial soils of the Missouri River floodplain at the northern edge of the Ozark Mountains and settled there to try their luck at farming. Soon the entire area was under cultivation. The homesteaders planted crops on every available patch of the fertile river soil, even right up to the bases of several bluffs that fronted the Missouri.

During the 1930s some workmen were preparing a foundation for a new home near the base of one of these bluffs across from the point where the Grand River joins the Missouri. As they were digging into the soft earth they uncovered a skeleton under a low mound. Lying beside the skeleton in this shallow grave was a small copper disc on which was engraved the image of the French flag. Subsequent investigation revealed that a French fur-trading company once based in St. Louis issued discs such as this one to their representatives.

A local medical doctor examined the skeleton and declared it to be that of a white man. It was assumed to be the skeleton of the Frenchman who had frozen to death during the conflict with the Indians in 1802.

The discovery of the skeleton generated renewed excitement about the possibility of a huge fortune in gold coins being cached in the area. Though no organized search had been undertaken since 1835, the tale of the buried treasure was widely known throughout the region and had long since entered the realm of Ozark folklore.

One day an old Indian woman arrived in the area and began making inquiries about the skeleton. Her forefathers had often told her the story of the Indian siege and the great fight waged by the Frenchmen. She possessed a French gold coin of great antiquity and claimed she had some knowledge of the buried gold. For several days she searched many of the local bluffs but came away empty-handed.

Around 1940, a farmer plowed up a gold coin while working in his field within thirty yards of a low limestone bluff. The coin bore French inscriptions, and was dated 1796. After showing the coin to several people, the farmer learned it may have been part of the buried treasure he had often heard about as a child. He returned to his field to try to relocate his find but was never successful.

The residents of this part of the Ozarks still firmly believe in the existence of the buried copper kettle filled with gold coins. However, they are quick to point out that there is other wealth to be found here, wealth that to them is far more important than gold: the rich agricultural lands that earn many a livelihood, provide food, and keep the people in tune with the soil and nature. It is not important to them whether the gold is ever found. What is important is the harmony they have achieved with the land, the satisfaction of successfully working a piece of God-given ground and the peace that comes with that effort.

They also talk of the wealth of tales of the early days: tales of adventure, Indian battles, explorers, their ancestors who settled this land, and buried gold. They are proud of their heritage, which includes wonderful stories handed down to them—stories and tales of the region for old folks to relate to their grandchildren. The stories are many and are an enduring part of their culture.

The tales, they readily tell you, can be had for the asking. The gold, buried somewhere in a field near a limestone bluff, is still to be found.

The Lost Cave of Silver

In the year 1800, two friends living in St. Louis undertook
an adventure that led them to what may have been one of the
richest silver mines on the North American continent. Unfortunately, it also led to their death.

The pair, one a Frenchman and the other a black man, met
while working on the docks in St. Louis, where they unloaded
freight from the many boats that journeyed up the Mississippi
River from New Orleans.

Somehow they acquired an ancient map on which was
marked the location of a rich silver deposit in the Ozark Mountains. The silver mine was supposedly very rich and had been
worked for many centuries by the local Indians. One version of
this tale relates that the friends found the map tucked into the
pocket of a coat worn by a dead Indian they discovered near the
loading docks. Another claims one of the men won the map in a
poker game.

At any rate, the two men persuaded a local businessman to
finance an expedition into the remote Ozark Mountains to look
for the mine. The businessman agreed in exchange for a share
of the wealth. He outfitted the men with good riding horses, a
string of pack mules, and supplies to last for several weeks, and
they departed for the interior of the Ozarks.

The first two days of the journey were uneventful. The
Frenchman maintained a diary and would occasionally scribble
notes into it as they rode along.

On the third day of traveling, the men discovered they were
being followed by Indians who remained approximately a hun-

dred yards behind, apparently trailing them but obviously in no particular hurry to overtake them. The two friends decided to ride ahead at a faster pace and find a place to hide and let the Indians pass them. They guided their mounts and pack animals into a deep thicket of trees some distance away from the main trail, and when they felt it was safe to proceed they set out once again toward the area indicated on the map. They met Indians a few other times but were neither approached nor threatened by them.

A few days later, following the directions provided on the map, they came to the silver mine. It was not a mine at all, but rather a natural cavern. Sometime in the distant geological past a great earthquake had struck this region, shattering many of the rock strata, severely fracturing the interior of the cave, and exposing a large vein of almost pure silver ore. The vein was described in the Frenchman's diary as being six feet high and about a foot wide.

Evidence of prior mining of the silver lay all about the cave. The men also found a crude smelter in which the ore was apparently melted down and formed into ingots. Several skeletons were also inside the cave.

The two men explored the inside of the cave for several hours and then set about the business of preparing a camp. During the evening meal the Frenchman entered the experiences off the day in his diary.

During the next two weeks, the men dug about twenty-five pounds of pure silver from the rich vein. One evening as they were filling their packs with the ore, they spotted several Indians watching them from the nearby ridges. Fearing hostile action, the men decided they should abandon the area that same night. They returned to the cave and covered the entrance in the hope that others would not discover the silver. At nightfall they quietly broke camp and stole away in the darkness.

During their flight from the Indians, the two friends became lost. Instead of traveling along the trail that would lead them back to St. Louis, they found themselves several miles west of the silver cave. While they debated about the correct route, they noticed that the Indians were still trailing them.

Deciding they would have a better chance if they split up, the two men divided the silver and rode away in different directions.

The Frenchman continued to travel westward for two days and then circled toward the north, eventually coming upon a trail that led to St. Louis. On the afternoon of the third day on this trail, he came upon the body of his friend. The body was lying in the middle of the trail and had over twenty-five arrows protruding from it. The horse and pack mules were nowhere in sight.

The friend had been dead for only a short time and the Frenchman feared the Indians might be close by. Taking a few moments to enter the information in his diary, he mounted up and fled the area at a gallop.

That evening as he set up camp on a ridge several miles away, the Frenchman discovered he was surrounded by Indians who were slowly and deliberately closing in on him. Realizing he would soon meet death in the manner of his friend, he scribbled some final notes in his diary. As the Indians approached, he placed the diary and the map to the silver cave into a pocket in his coat and sat back to await his fate.

Several days later a party of trappers chanced upon his body. As they prepared to bury him they discovered the map and diary stuffed into the coat. Reading his final entry, they learned how he met his death at the hands of the Indians. There was a notation in the diary requesting anyone who ever found it to return it and the map to the businessman in St. Louis who financed the search for the silver cave.

Several days later when the trappers arrived in St. Louis, they turned the Frenchman's belongings over to the businessman. Discouraged by the fate of the two men he had backed, he was unwilling to organize another expedition into the hostile Ozark Mountains in search of the cave. After several months had passed he made the contents of the Frenchman's diary public.

The diary provided directions to the silver cave. It described a fast-flowing creek that gushed out of a limestone cliff and ran for some distance before joining a larger river flowing from the southwest. From the point of this confluence, the two men had traveled northwest for about seven miles to a small valley oriented north-south. From this valley they entered a narrow ravine between two tall bluffs. Deep in this ravine was the fabled cave of silver.

Researchers who have studied the diary and map believe the stream described is the Roaring River. The larger river that flows from the southwest can only be the White River. Thus the lost silver cave would be south of the settlement of White Rock.

Indian hostilities in the deep Ozarks prevented another search for the silver cave for several years and soon the matter was forgotten. Many years later when the diary and map were rediscovered, interest in the mine was renewed and several organized search parties entered the region.

While the directions to the lost cave of silver are clear and precise and should lead a searcher directly to the mouth of the cavern, a significant obstacle has intruded. The location described in the dead Frenchman's diary is now deep under the waters of Table Rock Lake.

Other Tales of
Treasure in Missouri

The Treasure in the Well

John Hankins was a successful farmer who grew corn and feed in one of the broad creek bottoms in the Missouri Ozarks. He and his wife lived modestly in a log cabin he had built. They had no children of their own, but two of Mrs. Hankins's brothers farmed nearby, and the Hankins cabin often was host to nieces and nephews for desserts and storytelling.

Hankins's farm made a decent profit year after year, and he and his wife lived well. He was able to make deposits in the bank at the nearest settlement each year from the sale of his crops and livestock, but he never completely trusted financial institutions to safeguard his money. He made the bank deposits at the insistence of his wife, but unknown to her he occasionally hid money in a secret location on the farm.

Early one morning Farmer Hankins finished breakfast and went to the barn to hitch the mower to his team of mules. Mrs. Hankins was clearing the breakfast dishes when she heard a commotion in the barn. She called out to her husband but received no response. Running to the barn she discovered Hankins lying next to one of the stalls, unconscious and bleeding from the head. Apparently one of the mules had kicked him as he tried to hitch up the mower.

As Mrs. Hankins dragged her husband from the barn he

opened his eyes and tried to speak to her. Though dazed and delirious, he pointed to the well near the house and muttered something about money. When his wife asked him what he meant he again waved an arm toward the well and repeated the word "money." Then he died.

With the help of her brothers, Mrs. Hankins continued to run the farm. One evening as she and her two brothers were seated around the kitchen table, she related her husband's dying words about the well and the money. The next morning the brothers went out to the old well to examine it.

The well had been hand-dug by Hankins many years earlier and the water level could be seen at a depth of about twenty feet. A handmade oak bucket was raised and lowered by means of a sturdy windlass. One of the brothers, seated on the old bucket, was lowered into the well. As he descended he examined the stone sides for hiding places but found the entire wall solidly mortared. When he reached the water line he probed the bottom with a stick and again found nothing. They ultimately decided that Farmer Hankins must have been delirious and didn't know what he was saying.

The following week the well was covered over, the windlass taken down, and a hand pump installed to make the drawing of the water easier for Mrs. Hankins. The old oak bucket was taken to the barn and hung from a nail near the stall where Farmer Hankins was kicked by a mule.

One day about a year later one of the Widow Hankins's brothers arrived at the farm to help with the planting. He brought along his two young sons, who found the old barn a wonderful place to play. The boys entertained themselves in the barn loft playing games in the loose hay stored there.

Eventually tiring of their game, they were climbing down the ladder when one of them accidentally knocked the oak bucket from the nail on which it had hung for the past year. When the bucket hit the floor of the barn, one of the metal bands holding it together slipped off and the bucket came apart. Lying among the pieces were twenty twenty-five-dollar gold coins!

When the brother examined the old bucket he discovered it

had a false bottom in which the gold coins had been concealed. On being told of the discovery, the Widow Hankins realized that her late husband was attempting to tell her about the hidden gold in the bucket hanging in the well.

The Pot of Gold

The Civil War was responsible for many tragedies. Well over half a million men were killed in battle, and many thousands more returned home shattered and confused as a result of their violent experiences.

One such man was a veteran of the bloody Battle of Wilson's Creek. The atrocities he witnessed during this fight left him so crazed that he was eventually released from his military duties and returned to his home in Cedar County.

The soldier spoke incoherently yet continuously about a buried pot of gold near a church. At first a few people were interested in the story, but they soon became convinced the poor ex-soldier had truly lost his mind and they paid less and less attention to him.

Several years passed and the veteran slowly improved. He was eventually able to hold down a job and provide adequately for his family. His memory of the buried pot of gold also became increasingly clear.

He recalled that he and his two closest friends, on joining the army, agreed to pool their life savings and bury it in an old iron kettle until the war was over. During this time there were no banks in the area, so it was common for people to bury their wealth.

The three of them filled the pot nearly to the top with twenty-dollar gold pieces. With great difficulty, the three men managed to carry the heavy kettle to a church near the small settlement of Church Hollow and bury it in the graveyard. Then they carved a map showing the location of the buried kettle on a nearby flat stone.

The army veteran later learned that the two friends had been killed in the war and left no surviving relatives. He returned to the graveyard at the Church Hollow settlement to dig up the kettle but could not remember the exact place where it was buried. He searched for the flat rock on which the map was carved and discovered it had been moved, thus making the directional notations useless.

Somewhere in the old graveyard, next to a church that has long since fallen down, rests an iron kettle filled with gold coins.

The Lost Jack Fork Copper Mine

Gold and silver are not the only riches to be found in the Ozark Mountains. During the 1850s, a man named John Slater discovered a rich copper deposit and mined over fifty thousand dollars worth of the ore.

John Slater had heard many stories of gold and silver being discovered in the Ozarks and decided to try to find some for himself. He confined his prospecting to an area near the Current River about four miles above the mouth of Jack's Fork Creek. He had no luck finding gold or silver, but he accidentally discovered a rich deposit of copper.

Slater investigated the possibilities of filing a claim on the land where the copper deposit was located but found that it already belonged to someone else. Afraid of relinquishing his discovery, he filed a claim on an adjacent parcel of land and secretly worked the copper mine.

For four years Slater dug copper ore out of the ground and ferried it downriver, where it was eventually sold in New Orleans. Records there indicate he was paid over fifty thousand dollars for his crudely refined copper.

Slater was destined to be foiled, however. During this period the United States government sent representatives into the Ozark Mountains to conduct a formal survey of the land. The survey revealed that Slater's official claim was actually on land that belonged to someone else. An error had been made when Slater filed on the claim, but the U.S. survey was the final word on the matter and Slater was told to relinquish his claim. Fearful that contesting the claim might lead to the discovery of the copper mine, Slater decided to shut down his operation and abandon the area for a time. He covered the entrance to the mine and removed all evidence of mining. He then moved to St. Louis, intending to live there until he could return to the Jack's Fork area and purchase the land on which the mine was located.

Unfortunately, Slater died in St. Louis before he had a chance to carry out his plan. No trace of his copper mine has ever been found.

Fur Trapper's Lost Silver Coins

For many years the trapping of beaver and other fur-bearing animals in the Ozark Mountains provided a good living for the hardy souls who dared risk life and limb in country that was favored by hostile Indians and bandits on the run from the law.

As the nineteenth century drew to a close, however, the demand for furs dropped considerably. As a result, trapping decreased dramatically to the point where only a handful of persistent men entered the mountains each year to harvest pelts.

One of the more successful of these trappers was a Frenchman named Boucher who settled in the area of West Plains, Missouri. Boucher built a sturdy log cabin and moved his wife and daughter into it.

During the winter of 1901-02, Boucher purchased additional traps and supplies and set about laying trap lines in the hope that this would be his most profitable year. The winter was colder than normal and snow fell nearly every day. As a result the coats of the animals were thick and full and Boucher believed they would surely bring a good price come spring.

When spring arrived, Boucher loaded his pelts onto several pack animals and departed for the trading post at nearby Cape Girardeau. As he suspected, his pelts sold for top dollar. With his money, he purchased supplies and returned to his homestead with four hundred silver dollars jangling in his saddlebags.

On the second day of his journey home, Boucher noticed two men following him. He immediately suspected they knew about the money he carried in his saddlebags and were intent on robbing him. He believed the men would wait until he made camp for the night and then try to kill him and take the money. Boucher decided to foil the would-be bandits and, instead of stopping for the night, he pushed on toward his cabin in the hope of reaching it around dawn of the next day.

Just after dawn, Boucher was only three miles from his cabin when he spotted the two men who had been following him. The men were now approaching the trapper at a gallop, quickly narrowing the distance between them and their quarry. Boucher quirted his own mount and pack animals and rode hard toward the cabin.

Riding up to the front door, Boucher called his wife outside and told her he was being pursued and to act as if she didn't know him. He said he was going to ride over to the pond to bury the money and then circle back after the pursuers had left. Boucher then disappeared into the woods, riding toward the pond about a quarter of a mile away.

Within minutes the two men rode up to the cabin and called the inhabitants out. Boucher's wife came out onto the porch, her small daughter clutching at her apron. The men asked her if she had seen anyone ride by and she replied that one man had passed by earlier without stopping. They tipped their hats to her and rode on.

For the rest of the day and all that night Mrs. Boucher awaited her husband's return. When he had not arrived by dawn, she walked all the way to West Plains to get help. After hearing her story, several men volunteered to organize a search party.

The search centered near the pond, but nothing was ever found—no horses, no money, no Boucher. The trapper was never seen again.

What happened to Boucher? Did the pursuers catch him before he had a chance to hide the money? Was he killed? Many people believe the Frenchman buried the money before he was overtaken by the robbers. They suspect that Boucher was killed and his body hidden and his horse and pack animals stolen. They also believe that buried near the pond is an old rotted saddlebag containing four hundred silver dollars.

Hidden Treasure near Springfield

In the early 1930s a prominent Springfield family came into possession of a mysterious letter that described a cave in the region containing a huge Spanish treasure. The letter was written in Delverte, Mexico, and dated May 10, 1858. With great difficulty it was translated into English, and the Springfield *News and Leader* published it in July 1935. Here are the entire contents of that letter:

José Carozzo:
Go to what is now called Springfield,
Greene County, Missouri. It is a village about
twenty miles up the James River above the
old Spanish town of Levarro. Leave the
James River and go to Springfield. It has an
open square in the center. There is an old
road or trail that leaves from the southwest
corner of the square and runs southwest.
Follow this about two and one-half miles.
You will come to a dim road running east and
west. Go west on this road about a half-mile
and you will come to a big spring, some big
timber, and two or three old cabins.
If you look carefully, you will find some
sinks in the ground about four hundred paces
southwest of the big spring, and across the
creek there is a bluff. About three hundred
paces from the center of the bluff and down
the creek, there is another spring, not so
large as the first. Somewhere near the center

of the bluff, and fronting north on the creek, was the main entrance to the cave. It was filled up and covered by a big stone and there are three turkey tracks carved on the stone in a straight line east and west, and two of the same above. Remove this stone and also the filling for twelve or thirteen feet, and you will find a passage that descends for about twelve feet. When you reach the bottom of this descent, you will find a passage bearing nearly south. A little farther on you will find one running southeast, a little farther one running southwest. This is a false passage about thirty feet in length. It was cut to reach a deeper passage coming under the creek from the south side. It was abandoned when the new entrance was made.

This one you follow is the one running nearly south and dips down. You follow this until you enter a large room being used to work as a smelter to make bullion and Spanish money. The tools are there. My father and brother worked there years ago, and they have taken some from there after the Spanish left that country. There is plenty more for a dozen people, and more in sight.

If you cannot find it by these directions, you follow the creek that runs through Springfield and runs southwest. Follow it out to the flat or bottom where you will find a big spring, and just beyond the big spring about three hundred paces there is another creek coming into this creek a little south of east, and it comes together a little north of the east bluff where the cave is, dividing this bluff opposite the big spring and the bluff where the creek runs together. The creek here runs a little south of west.

I think the entrance to the mines was near the center of the bluff, on the north side, fronting the creek and above high water. When you leave the east and west dim road, there are three large oak trees. They are marked: The first tree is marked with a turkey foot; the second tree with two turkey feet; and the third tree has two turkey feet cut on the north side of the tree and pointing south by west. The spring is on the south side of the creek. Four hundred and ninety-six paces from the spring, southwest on the south side of the creek, is the entrance to the mines on the north side of the bluff near the creek.

Be patient and you will find it as the above is described. There are three kegs of gold stored in a niche in the big room, covered with gravel and broken stones.

José, if you succeed in finding this, be on your guard as to Saville.

Interestingly, several years later another letter describing the exact same treasure was discovered. The latest letter, written in the 1890s, had different handwriting but provides essentially the same directions to the cave. The description of the treasure also matches that of the first letter.

Around 1939 yet another letter was found, again providing directions to the cave and the treasure. The letter had fallen into the hands of two men who were using it as a guide to locate the cave. Following the directions in the letter, they found the cave. They removed the stone covering the opening as well as the fill dirt. The interior of the cave closely matched the description in the letter and, though they claimed they conducted a thorough search, the men did not find any treasure.

Thirty Bags of Gold

In 1884 a man arrived at the settlement of Lanagan, Missouri, bearing an ancient map purporting to show where thirty bags of gold had been buried over a century earlier. The man was purposely vague about how he had come into possession of the map and provided inquirers only his name, which was Von Wormer.

Tales of buried gold in and around the Lanagan area are common even today. The stories vary according to their teller, but they all involve a group of Mexican miners passing through the area on their way to New Orleans in the early eighteenth century. Exactly where the miners came from was a mystery, but they were leading a pack train bearing thirty bags of gold ore. On approaching the place called Bear Hollow, the miners were attacked by Indians. The frightened Mexicans fought gallantly and succeeded in repelling the attack but suffered severe casualties. Half of the men were killed and most of the pack animals were killed or wounded.

During the night the Indians gathered in preparation for a dawn assault. Meanwhile, the miners were burying their dead comrades. Then they gathered the thirty bags of gold and stuffed them into a nearby deep crevice adjacent to a small stream.

Relieved of their burden, the surviving miners escaped during the night, hoping someday to return for the fortune in gold they had secreted in the rock crevice.

Armed with his map, Von Wormer searched the region around Bear Hollow and claimed to have found the graves of the slain Spaniards. He related that he had dug up several of the graves and discovered mining tools that had been buried with the dead men.

The map was vague about the precise location of the rock crevice in which the thirty bags of gold were cached. It also appeared to Von Wormer that severe erosion during the past century had modified the little valley to the degree that it bore scant resemblance to what was sketched on the map. Unable to locate the gold, Von Wormer left the area, never to be seen again.

In 1928, another man arrived in Lanagan looking for the thirty bags of gold. This man was also in possession of a well-worn map and he spent a great deal of time scouring the Bear Hollow area. After two weeks of searching he returned to Lanagan, where it was learned he was the son of Von Wormer, who had searched for the gold forty-four years earlier!

Buried Jewelry at Neosho Falls

In 1870 a young man moved with his new bride into his family's ancestral home in Toledo, Spain. Over the next few weeks the newlyweds began remodeling the large old home. They had plans to raise a large family and wanted to remake the house according to their perceived needs.

While tearing down a wall in the house the young man discovered an old snuff box concealed within. Inside the box he found a weathered manuscript that gave a detailed account of his grandfather's search for El Dorado.

When the young man showed the manuscript to his mother she told him the story of his adventurous grandfather.

The grandfather had been a soldier and had traveled around the world. When he resigned his commission in the Spanish army he was not content to remain home doing nothing. Always intrigued by the Spanish search for El Dorado nearly two centuries earlier, he organized a party of adventurers to journey to the New World to take up where Coronado left off. He located a financial backer who provided the men with a fortune in jewels to be sold or traded along the way for supplies.

The men sailed to the New World but were never successful in discovering the fabled lost city of gold. Instead of digging up treasure, however, the party of adventurers was responsible for burying some. During one point of the journey, they decided to bury the container of jewelry and retrieve it at a later time. For reasons never explained the box of jewels was never recovered and the old manuscript provided a detailed description of its location:

> Proceed up the river called the Mississippi
> beyond where it is joined by the Red River,
> thence up the Arkansas River to the
> promontory known as Dardanelle Rocks.
> Passing this point proceed another one
> hundred miles upriver. From here, travel
> overland due north for fifteen days to an area
> wherein is located a waterfall, the only one
> to be found in the area. At a point halfway
> between the falls and a small creek to the
> north will be found a large flat rock with an
> arrow carved upon the surface. From this
> rock walk ninety paces east, the direction in
> which the arrow is pointed. Then walk ten
> paces south. The box of jewelry is buried
> here.

The young man who discovered the old manuscript in the snuff box journeyed to America in 1880 to search for the treasure. His trip up the Mississippi and Arkansas rivers was un-eventful, but when he reached the Ozark Mountains he became lost and wandered around for many days. He nearly died from starvation and exposure, but somehow, after several weeks of searching, found the flat stone on which the arrow was carved—though he failed to locate the buried jewelry.

Following the directions given in the old manuscript, one will arrive at a waterfall near Neosho, Missouri. A short distance to the north of the waterfall is Turkey Creek. In between these two landmarks supposedly lies the large flat stone with an arrow carved into it.

It is suspected that the grandson who searched for the box of jewelry had become disoriented as a result of the hardships he endured and had difficulty identifying the exact location at which the treasure was buried.

Given the many years that have elapsed since the box of jewelry was buried, it is likely that the image of the arrow has long since eroded away, or that the tangles of briars and brush in the little valley have covered the stone. The box of jewelry most likely still lies buried, approximately one hundred steps east of a point midway between Neosho Falls and Turkey Creek.

OKLAHOMA

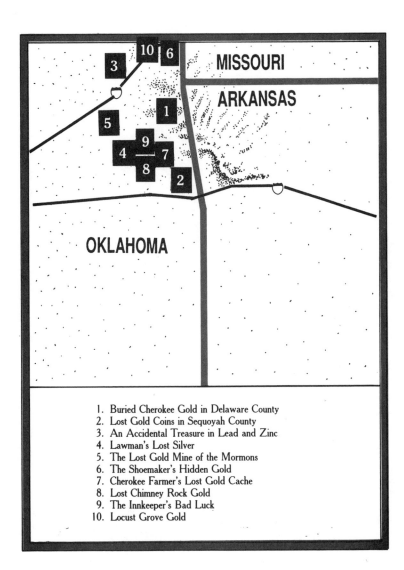

1. Buried Cherokee Gold in Delaware County
2. Lost Gold Coins in Sequoyah County
3. An Accidental Treasure in Lead and Zinc
4. Lawman's Lost Silver
5. The Lost Gold Mine of the Mormons
6. The Shoemaker's Hidden Gold
7. Cherokee Farmer's Lost Gold Cache
8. Lost Chimney Rock Gold
9. The Innkeeper's Bad Luck
10. Locust Grove Gold

Buried Cherokee Gold in Delaware County

In 1830, the United States forcibly removed thousands of Indians from their homelands in the southeastern part of the country, including Florida, Georgia, and the Carolinas. Affected were what came to be known as the Five Civilized Tribes: Cherokee, Choctaw, Chickasaw, Creek, and Seminole. Most of the Indians transplanted to Indian Territory (now Oklahoma) were provided with plots of land for farming. Many of them went willingly, but some were not anxious to vacate age-old homelands, the lands that had been settled and occupied by their ancestors for countless generations.

Many of the Indians who were not inclined to move had large farmsteads, some of them equal to the largest plantations that were to evolve in the South over the next few years. Some of the more prominent and powerful Indians owned slaves, sometimes numbering into the hundreds.

One such successful farmer was named Lacey Mouse. Mouse owned one of the largest Indian plantations in the Carolinas and was not enthusiastic about abandoning it for the journey to Oklahoma. He tried to bribe government officials to let him remain, but to no avail. Loading his possessions on several wagons and taking about thirty of his slaves, he left for Indian Territory.

Along the way, Mouse's slaves heard many stories about fiercely cold winters awaiting them in Oklahoma, and they feared they would freeze to death if they moved there. During

147

the trip several of them escaped. By the time Mouse reached the Mississippi River he decided to sell the dozen that remained.

Lacey Mouse always prided himself in having the strongest, hardest-working slaves in the land of the Cherokees. This "prime stock" brought top dollar and Lacey Mouse was paid off with a large bag of gold. He added this to the already large purse of wealth he had accumulated from years of farming in the Carolinas.

A few weeks later, he arrived at his parcel of land in the western part of Delaware County in the low rolling foothills of the Ozarks.

The story soon spread that Lacey Mouse was a wealthy man, but he always refused to discuss the amount of gold he possessed. Fearful that someone might try to take his gold from him, Mouse buried his fortune somewhere on his land one night.

Mouse operated a successful farm in Delaware County for many years and became one of the more prosperous Indians in the territory. He was respected by all who knew him and was eventually elected to some minor governmental position.

One evening in 1864, Lacey Mouse and a visiting relative had just completed their evening meal when they heard riders approach. Fearing trouble, Mouse sent the cook and housekeeper out the back door and encouraged his relative to hide under the bed. Mouse took a seat, lit his pipe, and waited to see what would happen. Within moments, three men stormed into the cabin and demanded Mouse's gold. Calmly, the Cherokee farmer refused. At this point one of the men bound him while the others searched the cabin for the gold. Remarkably, the outlaws never discovered the relative hiding under the bed.

When they couldn't find the gold, one of the men pulled a pistol from his belt and held the tip of the barrel to Mouse's head, telling him he would die if he didn't reveal the location of his wealth. Again Mouse refused, and was instantly shot through the head. After searching the cabin for a few more minutes, the outlaws fled, leaving the fearful relative cowering under the bed on which lay the dead Cherokee.

With the first light of morning, the relative came out from his hiding place, ran to the cabin of the nearest neighbor, and told the story of the murder. A group of men made an attempt to track the killers of Lacey Mouse, but lost the trail just a few miles from the farm. The men were never found.

The next morning, Lacey Mouse was laid to rest in a small plot on his farm.

Speculation immediately turned to the whereabouts of Lacey Mouse's wealth. Within days after the burial, local residents searched all over his farm to see if they could discover the Cherokee farmer's gold, but with no success.

Over the years the story of Lacey Mouse and his great wealth took on legendary proportions in the Indian Nations. Several organized attempts were made to locate the hiding place of Mouse's gold, but all ended in failure.

One day in 1943, according to a story told by an aged area resident, a hired hand was preparing some ground on what was once the Lacey Mouse farm. Using a two-horse team, the farm hand was plowing rows and breaking up an area of long dormant soil, readying it for a crop of corn.

The hand worked for most of the day, unhitched the animals, fed them, and put them up for the night. Just before sundown and just after supper, he walked out to the field to admire his work. Out near the middle of the field he saw the glimmer of the setting sun reflecting off several small objects. Curious, he walked into the field until he reached the spot. There, lying in the freshly turned rows, were several gold coins and the remnants of an aged leather sack.

The farm hand gathered up as many of the coins as he could find and returned to his cabin. At sunrise on the following day, he carried a shovel out to the spot where he found the gold coins. For the entire day he neglected the plowing and concentrated on digging up the ground where the coins were discovered. Though he dug two to three feet into the ground in a wide area, he was unable to locate more coins.

Did the hired hand accidentally stumble onto the location of Lacey Mouse's buried fortune in gold? Could his plow have snagged the leather sack just below the surface and carried it for several yards before eventually spilling its contents out onto the freshly plowed rows?

Several more attempts were made to locate the lost treasure of Lacey Mouse, but there is no evidence that his cache of gold coins was ever found.

Today, what was once the impressive farm of Lacey Mouse, prominent Cherokee landowner and farmer, is a brush- and briar-covered patch of land in the foothills of the Oklahoma Ozarks known as the Spavinaw Hills. Beneath the scrubby growth, perhaps by now entangled in the roots, may lie several more rotting leather sacks, stuffed with gold.

Lost Gold Coins in Sequoyah County

During the Civil War, soldiers from both the Union and Confederate armies sometimes occupied parts of Indian Territory. While no major battles were fought in this region, some aspects of the war did inflict some element of tragedy upon many of the area residents.

The Indians who lived in the region were, for the most part, neutral during the conflict—they had no interest in the philosophical differences between northern and southern white men. One advantage to having troops stationed in the Indian Territory, however, was that the region was made safer from the outlaw swarms that habitually sought refuge here. But once the troops withdrew, many desperadoes saw an opportunity to enter the area and renew depredations.

Usray was an Indian who lived with his son, daughter-in-law, and their one young child in the wooded foothills of the Ozark Mountains just east of Sallisaw. He had been granted a parcel of land on which he raised a few crops and some hogs and cattle. But Usray was best known for his fine horses. Anyone in the area who had need of a good work animal, a decent riding horse, or even a blooded racing horse would visit the Usray farm.

When the northern soldiers occupied this region, they occasionally found it necessary to replenish their supply of mounts. They soon learned that the best horseflesh to be obtained in these hills belonged to Usray. Several times they visited the Usray farm to buy mounts and pack animals, always paying in gold coin.

A frugal man, Usray had little need of the money and worldly goods, so he deposited the gold in a tin box that he kept hidden in his cabin, intending someday to give it all to his son.

As the war began to wind down, the Union soldiers gradually pulled out. At first Usray regretted the departure of the soldiers and the loss of the opportunity to do more business with them, but all things considered, he was happy to see them leave—happy, at least, until outlaws began moving back into the area.

Concerned that bandits might visit his farm now that he was without military protection, Usray pastured his best stock in a concealed meadow several hundred yards from the cabin, hoping the animals would escape the eye of roving horse thieves.

He was also concerned about the cache of gold under the floor of his cabin. He removed the tin box with the gold and added to it his wife's jewelry and a gold watch he had owned for many years. He wrapped the box in an old sheepskin rug and told his grandson he was going to bury it in the woods where it would be safe from marauders.

The little boy walked with Usray as far as the spring from which the family drew water. Telling the child to wait there, the old Indian disappeared into the hills. After about a half hour Usray returned to the spring and told the boy he had buried the box of gold and jewels where no one would ever find it.

That evening, as the Usray family sat down to their evening meal, they heard riders approach and call for whoever was in the cabin to come out. Fearing the newcomers might be outlaws, Usray hid his family under the floor of the cabin and walked outside to meet them.

Four men sat on horseback just beyond the small porch. They were a dirty lot and could be mistaken for nothing other than outlaws. The leader, who had a scarred face and unkempt hair spilling out from a wide-brimmed felt hat, spurred his horse a few steps toward the old man. He said he knew of the recent gold payment for the horses and demanded it be turned over immediately. He wore several pistols in his belt, and as he spoke with the old Indian, he gestured sharply with a rifle he carried in his right hand.

Calmly, Usray answered that he had earned that money and needed it for his family. He said he was not about to turn it over to worthless men too lazy to work for a living.

Angered, the leader asked once again for the money, warning Usray that if he did not turn it over he would pay with his life.

In response, Usray stood squarely on the porch and folded his arms across his chest in a gesture of defiance. Unafraid, he held the gaze of the outlaw.

At a signal from the leader, another of the group rode forward, threw a lasso over the old man, and yanked him off the porch and into the dirt. Tying the other end of the rope around his saddle horn, the outlaw dragged the Indian across the clearing to the edge of the woods near the spring. There the bandits pulled the old man to his feet and asked him once again for the gold, telling him he would hang if he didn't hand it over. Again Usray refused.

One member of the outlaw band adjusted the loop around Usray's neck while another tossed the opposite end over a low-hanging branch of a nearby oak tree. Together, they pulled the old man into the air and let him hang there for several seconds before releasing the rope and letting him drop to the ground. Dazed, Usray gagged and choked, trying to force air into his lungs.

By this time, Usray's grandson had crawled from his hiding place under the floor of the cabin and watched in horror as the bandits tortured his grandfather.

Several more times they hoisted the Indian, letting him feel the rope choking the life out of him. Just when it seemed he would surely die, they would drop him once again to the ground and repeat their demand. Still the old man refused to reveal the location of the gold.

One of the bandits removed Usray's moccasins and threatened to pull out his toenails. In response, the Indian spit on his tormentor. When they proceeded to remove his toenails, the old man did not give them the satisfaction of crying out, but stoically bore the pain.

Frustrated, the outlaw leader stabbed the Indian and had his compatriots hang his body from the limb.

The outlaws then turned their attention to the cabin. Ignoring the sobbing grandson, they turned over furniture and ransacked the small home until they were certain the gold was not there. The outlaws never discovered the frightened family members hidden under the wooden floor. Finding nothing of value in the cabin, they rode away.

When the outlaws were gone, the grandson informed the others and all came out from hiding. The boy told them what he had seen them do to his grandfather. They all went to the spring, cut the old man down, and cried over his body.

After the burial the next day, the grandson told the other members of the family about Usray's taking the tin box full of gold and jewels out into the wooded hills and burying it where "no one would be able to find it."

While Usray had no need for gold or money, he died protecting his wealth presumably so that his descendants would inherit it. But before he had the opportunity to tell his son where he had buried the gold and jewels, he lost his life. Several attempts were made to locate the hiding place of the Union gold payments to the old Indian, but history does not record that it was ever found.

An Accidental Fortune in Lead and Zinc

Patrick McNaughton was born and raised in the Tennessee hills in a family that was accustomed to poverty and hardship. He was one of seven children, and it soon became clear that he would have to strike out on his own so he would not be a burden to his mother and invalid father.

Since no work was available in the area, McNaughton walked all the way to Fort Smith, Arkansas, with no money in his pocket and only the clothes on his back. He was thirteen years old.

In Fort Smith he immediately found work as a laborer. By day he toiled at the loading docks on the Arkansas River and by night he slept in alleys and under porches. Frugal by nature, he refused to spend any more money than was necessary to survive.

In time the young McNaughton took a job with a freighter who hauled goods from Fort Smith to Springfield, Missouri. While thus employed, he learned to handle a wagon and team and was soon given the responsibility of hauling freight through the rugged Ozark Mountains. He continued to save his money with the intention of starting his own freighting business.

McNaughton's travels took him to new and exciting parts of the frontier West. He found work as a teamster and freighter in Arizona, Utah, and Texas and often delivered goods to mining camps. While visiting these settlements he learned to recognize gold and silver and eventually acquired the rudiments of prospecting from the miners he came to know.

The lure of the potential wealth to be found in precious ores in the western ranges appealed to the young man's sense of adventure, but his conservative nature and frugal approach to life kept him occupied with the security of hauling freight.

By the fall of 1877, Patrick McNaughton had grown to be a tall, rangy man. He was sturdy of build, known throughout many parts of the West as a competent freighter, and was typical of the tough and persevering individual the rugged frontier was known to spawn. Like many others of his day he sported a long handlebar moustache. He seldom wore anything but overalls, and a well-worn bowler covered his balding head.

Late October in 1877 found McNaughton carrying a load of freight from Sherman, Texas, to Kansas City, Missouri. After crossing the Red River into Oklahoma, he picked up an aged Indian he found walking along the road. The Indian explained to McNaughton that he was an elder in the Shawnee tribe and was trying to return to their lands near Vinita in northeastern Oklahoma.

Since the old man looked half-starved, McNaughton shared his rations with him and saw that he rested comfortably in the back of the wagon.

Eventually they arrived at the Shawnee reservation near Vinita, where they were greeted by members of the tribe. They welcomed the return of the elder and made plans to celebrate the event with a feast that evening. McNaughton was invited to attend. Itching to be on his way, the freighter nevertheless remained at the encampment and helped the Indians celebrate the return of one of their own.

The next morning, as McNaughton was readying his team, he was approached by the old Indian who invited the young man to walk with him for a while. The Indian expressed his gratitude to McNaughton for caring for him and transporting him back to his family. In appreciation, he said he wanted to share a secret of the Shawnees that would lead his new friend to great wealth and happiness.

The Indian told the freighter of the existence of a long-lost Spanish silver mine about a two-day wagon ride from the village. Occasionally, he said, several Shawnees at a time would journey to the mine and retrieve some of the bright metal from which they fashioned ornaments. He showed several of these ornaments to McNaughton, who judged them to be made from pure silver ore of the highest quality.

The Indian scratched the directions to the mine in the dirt, bade farewell to his new friend, and returned to the village.

As McNaughton continued on his journey to Kansas City, he pondered the tale related by the Indian. He was convinced the old man was telling the truth about the Spanish silver mine, but he was reluctant to give up the secure income of the freighting business to go chasing after silver. He thought about the times he visited the mining camps of the West, where he was often tempted to sell everything in order to search the mountains and streams for gold. The excitement of the lure of wealth and adventure fought with his conservative and frugal side. As he whipped his team along the trail he became more and more confused about what he should do.

By the time McNaughton had reached Seneca on the Oklahoma-Missouri line, he had made up his mind. After dinner at a small inn, he located a man who would haul the freight the rest of the way for him. Then he rented a buckboard and two strong horses to carry him and a wagonload of supplies to a remote part of the Oklahoma Ozark hills described by the old Shawnee Indian.

From Seneca, his trail took him westward into the unsettled regions along the Spring River in the land of the Peoria Indians. The trail was little used and the country was rugged, thus making passage difficult. To add to the problem, the autumn rains caused the rivers and creeks to swell, and several times McNaughton was forced to wait until the rains subsided and the streams were safe to cross. At the end of the fourth day, he arrived at the site described by the Indian. Remarkably, he said in later years, he was able to step from his buckboard and walk right up to an ancient shaft in a matter of a few moments.

As McNaughton walked throughout the area he came upon more shafts, eventually locating a total of twenty-three over a forty-acre area.

Knowing a little bit about mining, McNaughton noted that all of the shafts were round, dug in the manner of traditional Spanish mining. Several of them penetrated well over three hundred feet into the ground.

That evening as McNaughton set up camp in the dark, he pondered the fortune that awaited him on the morrow.

The next morning McNaughton began a systematic exploration of the mines. He fashioned several torches out of the tough grass that grew in profusion. He entered each of the shafts over the next few days seeking indications of silver.

In most of the tunnels he found great quantities of lead. He knew this was not unusual, for his experiences told him that silver was often found in association with lead deposits. McNaughton found evidence of silver mining in nearly all of the shafts, and he recovered several small nuggets of silver from the mining debris on the ground.

While McNaughton found abundant evidence that silver was indeed mined from these shafts, he was unable to locate a vein of the ore that appeared productive. For several days he continued to explore the ancient Spanish mines but found little to reward his efforts. Finally, he decided that whatever silver might have existed there had been long since mined out and further efforts would be fruitless.

McNaughton cursed his bad luck and began to regret the time lost from his freighting business. As he guided the buckboard along the return trail, his keen eyes scanned the surrounding hills, searching for some sign of silver. Now and then he would stop at a promising site and examine the rock more closely. He continued to find a lot of lead, but no silver.

As McNaughton rode along he realized he was doing what he always wanted to do. He became fired with the excitement of the search for wealth; it had taken hold of him and would not let go. While he worried about his freighting business, his heart was in the search for silver. It was obvious that a great amount of silver had been taken from the area. He knew there was still more silver in these hills and felt certain he could find it. Acting on a hunch, he stopped at the Peoria Indian agent headquarters and requested permission to do some prospecting on the Indian lands. The agent informed McNaughton of a law expressly prohibiting such activity in Indian country and turned him down. Frustrated, McNaughton returned the buckboard and team to Seneca. As soon as he could arrange for transportation, he left for his home in Sherman, Texas.

Once in Sherman, McNaughton enlisted the help of an influential rancher who in turn asked the Interior Department about gaining permission to prospect on Indian lands. Encouraged by the response, McNaughton journeyed to Washington, D.C., to meet with Interior Secretary Carl Schurz. Schurz was sympathetic to McNaughton's plea and granted permission to prospect, but specifically forbade the extraction of minerals from the Peoria land.

Encouraged, McNaughton arranged to purchase leases from the Peoria Indians and made preparations to begin his work. He invested the last of his savings in equipment and supplies in the hope of locating the wealth he believed lay beneath the limestone crust of the Ozark hills.

For weeks he searched, often doubling back to make certain he had not missed anything important, but the results were always the same. He continued to find plenty of lead but no silver. When his supplies finally ran out, McNaughton was discouraged and disheartened. As he was a man not accustomed to failure, this was a heavy blow to his self-esteem.

That night as he sipped coffee in front of his campfire, he pondered his luck. His thoughts kept returning to the great quantities of lead he had discovered during his search for silver. Suddenly he was struck with an idea. He would mine the lead!

The next morning McNaughton made another sweep of the area to inventory the amount of lead he might be able to extract when he made a fascinating discovery. Along with the lead he found great quantities of zinc. It wasn't silver, to be sure, but it could still earn him a fortune.

He returned once again to Texas to formulate plans to extract the lead and zinc from the Ozark hills. His main obstacle was the

Interior Department order banning all mining in the Peoria lands.

Not to be denied, McNaughton entered into several weeks of negotiations with Indian leaders and the federal government and was finally granted permission to dig. He borrowed money and purchased mining equipment. In a short time, he was realizing his dream as lead and zinc were being mined.

McNaughton called his organization the Peoria Mining Company after the local Indian tribe, and he soon had over three hundred men working for him. Eventually a town, named Peoria, sprang up complete with hotel, post office, and school. Within weeks several other mining concerns moved into the area, obtained rights, and began extracting lead and zinc. The year was 1891 and the northeastern Oklahoma Ozarks were experiencing a lead and zinc mining boom.

But with so many shafts penetrating the crust of the hills and so much of the mineral being extracted, it was inevitable that the boom was not to last for long. The huge deposits were soon exhausted, and eventually one company after another packed up and left. By 1896, five years after McNaughton sank his first shaft, Peoria, Oklahoma, was on its way to becoming a ghost town.

Patrick McNaughton never realized the wealth he originally anticipated from his mining adventure, but he earned enough to live comfortably for the rest of his life. He never located the silver he originally set out to find, but rather by accident reaped a fortune in lead and zinc. As a result of McNaughton's efforts, several other sites in northeastern Oklahoma, southeastern Kansas, and southwestern Missouri were prospected for lead and zinc and, over the years, billions of dollars worth of these minerals were mined.

Lawman's Lost Silver

During the last half of the nineteenth century, the re-
motely settled area known as Indian Territory was rapidly becoming a haven for outlaws and renegades. For many years,
organized law enforcement stopped at the western border of
Arkansas and the outlaw element was relatively safe from pursuit. Hundreds of the lawbreakers found refuge in the vast and
lawless spaces of what eventually became the state of Oklahoma.

The rugged Ozark hills and valleys where Indian Territory,
Arkansas, and Missouri came together afforded some of the best
hiding places, and criminals were densely concentrated in these
western reaches of the Ozarks.

Occasionally groups of outlaws would leave this refuge to
make raids on farms and travelers in Arkansas and Missouri,
killing, robbing, and raping in the process. They would retreat to
the sanctuary of the Oklahoma Ozarks before lawmen could
arrive at the scene.

The situation became so critical that federal marshals were
eventually ordered into these remote parts of Indian Territory to
capture known outlaws and return them to stand trial at Judge
Isaac Parker's court in Fort Smith.

Dozens of United States marshals and deputies operated
throughout much of the eastern part of the territory until Oklahoma achieved statehood in 1907. Given the wild and somewhat
primitive conditions under which these men were forced to
work, and given the inherent dangers associated with their task,
they compiled an impressive record during the years they were

active.

Among the more efficient and effective of these heroic lawmen was Deputy United States Marshal Joseph Payne. Payne was assigned to Judge Parker, who in turn assigned him to cover the wild and hazardous Ozark region of Indian Territory. In the first few months Payne gained a reputation as a competent lawman. Because of his outstanding record of bringing criminals to justice, Parker gave him the most difficult assignments.

In the spring of 1881, Payne was sent into the hills a few miles south of Tahlequah, some twenty miles west of the Arkansas border, to track and apprehend perpetrators of a raid on a farm near the state line. The outlaw group numbered five, and it was a testimony to Judge Parker's confidence in Payne that he sent him out alone.

Payne tracked the outlaws for several days through the hills and valleys of this western fringe of the Ozarks until the trail led him to a narrow valley sheltered by steep bluffs. He decided not to enter the valley alone, believing the sensible thing to do would be to return to Fort Smith for reinforcements.

During the several days of tracking, he had exhausted most of his rations. As the area through which he was traveling was full of deer, he decided to do some hunting and smoke some meat. Staking out his horse in a narrow meadow, he took his rifle and followed fresh deer tracks into a promising-looking stand of trees in a nearby valley. The little valley had been carved out by a small, fast-flowing stream that ran into the Illinois River about a mile to the west.

Payne spotted several deer but none presented a clear shot. After hunting for two hours and not having anything to show for his efforts, he was frustrated and tired. He paused by the stream to rest for a while.

Payne removed one of his boots to check for wear on the sole when a glint of color from the stream attracted his attention. Replacing the boot, Payne walked over to the shallow creek and observed a vein of color three feet wide bisecting the limestone rock of the stream bed. The vein disappeared under the banks on each side.

Payne entered the creek and, using his knife, probed at the vein. It had a soft texture and he was able to gouge out several small pieces.

Returning to the bank, Payne examined his find and was surprised to discover it was pure silver. He returned to the creek, dug into the banks on both sides, and found that the vein continued for several yards in each direction.

The apparent high quality of the ore, the thickness of the vein, and the fact that it extended a considerable distance just below the shallow soil layer gave Payne reason to believe he had discovered a very rich lode of silver.

Payne immediately abandoned the deer hunt and returned to Fort Smith as fast as he could ride. He requested and received leave from his duties as deputy marshal and returned to his find.

On this trip Payne brought along a hand drill that he used to probe the depth of the vein. The drill was four feet long, and he found silver at that depth just as pure as that dug from the surface. Payne estimated he had several tons of the rich ore under his feet.

Payne was aware of the federal restrictions on prospecting and mining on Indian lands, so he decided to proceed cautiously.

In Fort Smith, he made discreet inquiries about the possibility of obtaining permission to mine in Indian Territory, but he was discouraged at every turn. He knew it would not be possible to do any kind of large-scale mining without being detected and he was unwilling to risk the penalties to which he would be subjected should he be discovered.

When he could find the time, Payne returned to his secret location and dug enough silver to fill a saddle bag. He never carried much of the ore at any one time for fear of arousing suspicion.

His law enforcement duties often took him far from his silver, and sometimes several months would pass before he could return and dig some of the ore. On one of the rare occasions he was able to visit the site he accidentally rode into an outlaw camp. Gunfire was exchanged, and Payne was lucky to escape with his life. The incident discouraged him from returning for nearly two years, and when he did he remained nervous and frightened the entire time.

During one of his infrequent trips to the creek, Payne decided to conceal the vein of silver so it could not be discovered by others who might pass this way. He felled several large trees across the creek and constructed a makeshift dam to divert the path of the flowing water. Then he covered the vein with several smaller limbs and forest debris. As many times as he had been to this site, he believed he would have no trouble relocating it.

With increasing frequency, Payne's law enforcement assignments took him far from his silver for long periods of time. The Indian Territory continued to fill with outlaws, and marshals were working longer and harder trying to bring criminals to justice.

Years passed before Payne found an opportunity to return to the vein of silver, but when that opportunity finally arrived, he became ill and unable to travel.

His illness grew progressively worse and, as he lay close to death, he told a close friend of the existence of the silver in the remote valley of the Oklahoma Ozarks. He described the area near the creek, noting certain landmarks. He also drew a map showing how to reach the site.

Joseph Payne never recovered from his illness and died in 1904. Several weeks later the friend tried to locate the silver. Using Payne's map, he ventured into the Ozarks in search of a particular narrow valley with a fast-flowing stream.

For weeks the friend searched the hills south of Tahlequah but found the map useless. While Payne had been able to ride straight to the creek, he was unable to communicate the directions adequately on his map. Eventually the friend gave up and burned the map.

If Joseph Payne was correct, then somewhere in the low hills in the western part of the Ozarks just south of Tahlequah lies a fortune in pure silver. Payne claimed discovery of this supposedly rich deposit but was unable to mine it. Others may have searched for it but if they discovered it they kept it a secret. Some searchers believe that Payne's improvised dam across the creek might have rearranged the channel so that all evidence of the silver is now hidden under several inches of soil.

Today this area is popular with deer hunters and it is likely that some of them enter the little valley in search of game, just as Joseph Payne did over one hundred years ago. They may be tracking game across the very layer of soil that covers the lawman's lost silver.

The Lost Gold Mine
of the Mormons

During the first two decades of the twentieth century,
Pryor, Oklahoma, was the setting for both good times and bad.
Residents of this small town in the northeastern part of the state
just west of the foothills of the Ozarks, boasted that it was one of
the most progressive cities in Oklahoma. At the same time,
however, outlaws of one stripe or another called it home. Shoot-
ings, knifings, and robberies were common, and the comings
and goings of the lawless element were an unfortunate fact of
life in Pryor. While the local Chamber of Commerce extolled the
wonders of the Oklahoma hills, the town itself retained the
atmosphere of wilder days when it was Indian Territory.

There was one aspect of the town, however, that nearly
everyone pointed out with pride: the Pryor Orphans' Home.
Even though economic times were hard and many were without
work, the home stayed open as a result of donations from
citizens and various churches.

The Reverend W.T. Whittaker had founded and operated the
orphanage, and it was largely due to his persuasive manner that
the institution was able to pay its bills on a regular basis. When
not on the premises, the Reverend Whittaker rode a carriage
throughout the county pleading for contributions. He worked
seven days a week at keeping the doors of the home open.

One morning in the spring of 1921, Reverend Whittaker was
running errands in town and stopped at the post office. He found
among the mail an envelope with an Ohio postmark. Curious, he

tore it open and read the letter.

The writer, an Ohio resident, told Whittaker that he had been provided his name and address by one who attested to his honesty and dependability. The writer also stated that his source of information claimed that Whittaker was familiar with the Spavinaw Hills region of the Ozarks several miles east of Pryor. Following this introduction, the letter continued with an interesting story.

The letter writer had recently learned of a very rich gold mine in the Spavinaw Hills. He also claimed he had maps of the area and would pay Whittaker a large sum of money if he would guide the Ohioan into the region and provide him with men to help excavate the gold should they locate it.

Whittaker, foreseeing the opportunity to acquire funds for the orphans' home, decided it might be worthwhile to participate in the gold-hunting venture. He returned home and wrote a letter to the Ohioan tentatively agreeing to the proposition and requesting more details.

The return mail brought the story. The Ohioan had recently come into possession of the diary of a man who had worked in the gold mine many years earlier. The man was one of twelve Mormons who were exploring the Spavinaw Hills in search of a suitable location for a settlement when they accidentally discovered a rich vein of gold in an outcrop of the weathered limestone that forms these hills. Believing they were sent by God to discover this gold, the Mormons immediately established a tiny settlement and set to the task of mining and smelting the ore. The gold was to be shipped to Salt Lake City, to help fund the construction of the temple.

Day after day, from dawn until late in the evening the men worked in the mine, stopping only to eat, rest, and conduct worship services. They removed tons of rock from the shaft, separated the ore from the matrix, and fashioned eighteen-inch ingots in a crude homemade smelting operation.

After several months of hard work, the Mormons had accumulated several hundred bars of the gold ore, which they stacked along one side of the mine shaft. They planned to purchase mules and carry the gold to Salt Lake City once the vein of ore was exhausted.

The operation was not without trouble. Repeated encounters with outlaws and ruffians as well as occasional gunfights forced the Mormons to abandon their mining temporarily. Because of the increased harassment, the men decided it would be best to cover and conceal the mine shaft, sealing the gold ingots within. Having done so they departed, intending to return when the outlaw menace was eliminated.

For reasons unknown, the Mormon miners never returned to the valley to reclaim their gold. Years passed, and the story of the lost Mormon mine came into the possession of the letter writer from Ohio by way of the diary of one of the miners.

Convinced of the authenticity of the tale, Whittaker spent the next few days lining up men to accompany him and the Ohioan on an expedition into the Spavinaw Hills. Once this was accomplished, Whittaker decided it was time to write to the man and tell him everything was ready to proceed and to come at once.

Bad luck befell the good reverend, however, for on his way home to write the letter he was stricken with a heart attack. Whittaker lay in a coma for several days, unable to speak. Finally, in the presence of family and friends, he died.

Several weeks later, members of his family discovered the correspondence from the Ohio writer. Unaware that the man was awaiting a return letter from Reverend Whittaker, the family ignored the matter. It is presumed that the Ohioan believed Whittaker was not interested in the project and so he apparently never wrote again.

Over the next few years the story of the Lost Mine of the Mormons surfaced from time to time, and men would enter the Spavinaw Hills with the hope of locating the lost cache. Searchers for the mine discovered evidence of a small abandoned settlement in one of the valleys. Not far from this discovery they found the remains of a primitive smelter. The searchers spent several days in the area but could not find the mine.

More time passed and the city of Tulsa developed plans to create a reservoir on the Neosho River to be used as a water supply. Once the dam was constructed, water backed into several of the secluded valleys in the Spavinaw Hills.

Many who have searched for the lost gold mine of the Mormons believe that the actual site of the diggings was covered when the valley was filled to form Spavinaw Lake, forever covering the hundreds of golden ingots stacked against the walls of the old mine shaft.

The Shoemaker's Hidden Gold

In the summer of 1870, an elderly German arrived in Indian Territory leading two mules. His ragged and dirty appearance suggested he had obviously been traveling for a long time, and the mules appeared weary from the burden of the heavy loads they carried.

The old fellow stopped at several of the farmhouses in the area and offered to work in return for some food and a place to sleep. He made it known that he was a cobbler and soon found plenty of work mending the boots and shoes of nearly everyone in the region. The old man was friendly and got along well with the locals, but most of the time he preferred to be alone. At times he appeared somewhat secretive, and when anyone approached his mules he would chase them away. Once, as he was repacking a load on one of the animals, someone reported seeing several leather sacks filled with gold coins.

The old shoemaker had been in the area for several weeks when he finally set up residence on a parcel of land fronting the Spring River just a few miles northeast of present-day Miami, Oklahoma. No other white residents were nearby, and his closest neighbors were members of the Piankashaw Indian tribe, a small group of Indians that had been moved to the territory from Kansas only three years earlier.

The shoemaker constructed a rude cabin from native material. Those who chanced near his residence were greeted in a friendly manner by the German, but he remained secretive and never allowed anyone in his house.

One day a traveler arrived at a nearby settlement and spotted the old German purchasing a few items at the trading post. The traveler related to several of the citizens that he had known the shoemaker many years earlier in the old country. He said the German came from a wealthy and influential family but, for reasons unknown to anyone, had became a cobbler, traveling from village to village repairing boots and shoes. After working thus for many years, the German journeyed to the United States. He landed somewhere on the East Coast and immediately set out for the West. He worked his way across the country performing odd jobs and cobbling. Most of those who encountered him found him somewhat eccentric but harmless.

The traveler also said that the shoemaker was rumored to have carried much of his family's wealth with him when he came to America.

Aside from his infrequent visits to the nearest settlement, hardly anyone encountered the old shoemaker save for a few of the Piankashaws living nearby. The German became close friends with one particular young member of the tribe and occasionally invited him to share a meal. One day, as the two sat on the ground in front of the cabin, the shoemaker confided in the Indian that he had great wealth in gold coins. He showed the young Piankashaw a large tin box in which he claimed his fortune was kept and confessed to him that he was unable to sleep at night for fear that someone would steal his treasure. The Indian suggested to the shoemaker that he hide his gold someplace where no one could find it.

The German considered this idea for several days and finally decided to follow the advice of the Indian. For several days, the shoemaker explored the area around his cabin until he finally located a suitable hiding place.

Near the point where Rock Creek flows into the Spring River is a high limestone bluff containing several deep crevices. Entering one of these narrow cracks in the rock, the shoemaker followed it until it became too dark to see. Fashioning a torch from grasses that grew along the creek, he re-entered the crevice and, inching forward on his stomach for several dozen yards, followed it until he came to a large room in which he was able to stand to his full height.

The next day, with the help of his mules, the shoemaker carried his fortune to the crevice. After several trips, he finally succeeded in sliding the tin box and his many sacks of gold coins through the narrow crevice and into the room. Using the light from a torch, he arranged the tin box in one corner of the room and filled it with the sacks of gold. Then he crawled back through the narrow opening and returned to his cabin. Several days later he told his young Indian friend what he had done and related that he had slept peacefully for the first time in weeks.

A year passed and the old shoemaker grew weak from a sickness that caused great fits of coughing. The sickness ravaged his body and left him unable to rise from his bed without difficulty. His Piankashaw friend tended to him as best he could, but it was clear the old man was dying.

One day when the Indian brought some food to the old shoemaker he found him nearly dead. The old German pulled the Indian close to him and whispered the secret location of his hidden gold. He told the young Piankashaw that he wanted him to have his wealth for being his friend and for caring for him during his sickness. He told the Indian the money was to be used to benefit his tribe.

A few days later the old man died. The Piankashaws buried him next to his cabin and conducted a simple service in the manner of the Indians.

One morning a few days following the burial, the Indian set out in search of the shoemaker's hidden gold. He easily located the confluence of Rock Creek and the Spring River and immediately spotted the limestone bluff described by the old man.

In searching the bluff, the young Indian found many crevices in the rocky face, but none that yielded a fortune in gold coins.

Many times the Indian searched the area now known as Devil's Promenade, but the crevice through which the old shoemaker moved his fortune eluded him. After several weeks of searching with no success, the Indian gave up, and the story of the old shoemaker's lost gold persisted as legend among his tribe for over a century.

In 1979, Weldon Bobcat, a Kiowa Indian who has spent a lot of time around the Spring River, related an interesting story. Several boys had been playing near Devil's Promenade a few summers before when one of them entered a narrow crevice he found in the face of the bluff. Crawling flat on his stomach, the youth discovered the crevice extended far into the cliff for several yards. When he exited, he told his companions that it appeared the crevice opened into a room large enough to accommodate several people, but he confessed to being afraid of the numerous nests of spiders through which he would have had to crawl in order to reach the chamber.

It is possible that the boy had accidentally discovered the hiding place of the old shoemaker's gold, but being unaware of the legend, he saw no need to enter the chamber where the old tin box filled with gold coins has rested quietly for over a century.

Cherokee Farmer's Lost Gold Cache

Jim Bobb was one of several children of a Cherokee family that farmed a small patch of land near Baumgarner Hollow in the Ozark hills, several miles east of Tahlequah, Oklahoma. The small farm was granted to the elder Bobb during the settlement of the Cherokee Indians into this area, and he made a decent living raising hogs and growing corn in the good river bottom soil. Life was generally good for the Bobb family.

Jim Bobb, unlike his siblings, possessed a wanderlust and often spoke of wanting to visit faraway places. When news about the California gold fields reached this isolated area of Indian Territory, Jim Bobb packed his few meager belongings and left, heading westward to seek the wealth he dreamed of.

He toiled for two years in the California Rockies, panning gold from hundreds of the small glacially fed streams that pour down out of the mountains. He experienced some successes and was careful to save as much as was practical. By the time he returned home to the farm in Oklahoma, he brought with him a large pack filled with gold dust and nuggets.

Jim Bobb moved in with his family and resumed working on the farm. With some of his newfound wealth, he gradually added to the family holdings by purchasing adjacent acreage, putting together a large and efficient farm. In time he married, built a stout cabin on the property, and was soon the father of a fine son he named Robin.

As time passed, Jim Bobb, with Robin's able assistance, developed a fine herd of cattle, expanded the corn fields, and turned the family farm into a very profitable enterprise. Income from the Bobb farm was more than adequate, and the profits were added to the already large pile of gold dust and nuggets kept hidden under a floor board inside the cabin.

Robin Bobb grew to manhood and maintained a deep interest in the farm. As his father grew feeble with age, Robin took on more of the responsibility for the operation and proved capable of carrying on the family tradition. By the time Jim died, the wealth that had accumulated under the cabin floor was so great that the son decided it was necessary to find a new location for it.

Having no experience with banks and bankers, Robin Bobb simply elected to find a suitable hiding place some distance from the farm, a place to which he could easily return and extract some of the gold when necessary. He removed the cache of wealth from under the floor of the cabin and stuffed it into a large old cooking pot, which he wrapped in heavy canvas. Securing the heavy load onto a pack horse, Robin Bobb rode into some low rocky hills of the Ozark Mountains just east of the Illinois River. Locating what he believed to be a secure spot, he concealed the cooking pot full of gold and returned to his farm.

More years passed and, as Robin Bobb told the story, there was no need to retrieve any of the hidden gold, for the farm prospered and provided well for him and his family. Neighbors had heard stories of the fortune Jim Bobb brought back from the California gold fields in his youth, but the farmer always refused to discuss it with anyone. In fact, Robin Bobb never revealed the location of the hidden gold to anyone in his own family.

One autumn, Robin Bobb suddenly became ill and died within a few weeks. Though he left no directions to the hidden gold cache, several family members undertook a search for it in the general area they believed it to be. But somewhere in the hills east of Tahlequah, the great wealth of Robin Bobb remains unclaimed to this day.

Lost Chimney Rock Gold

Chimney Rock, a tall spire of sedimentary rock and well-known Oklahoma Ozark landmark, was once the site of an extended gun battle between outlaws and a pursuing posse. This prominent landform, some five miles southeast of Tahlequah, casts a shadow over two mule loads of gold buried somewhere near its base.

The gold that was supposed to have been buried near the base of Chimney Rock came from Louisiana. Six desperadoes rode into a northern Louisiana town, robbed a storehouse in which the gold had been kept, and fled north and east toward Indian Territory, then a well-known haven for outlaws.

Within moments of the robbery, a dozen citizens of the town saddled up, secured provisions, and rode out in pursuit of the outlaws. For several days and nights the chase continued, with the pursuers occasionally getting close enough to the bandits to fire shots. The outlaws, leading two pack mules loaded down with the gold, would somehow manage to elude the persistent Louisianans and the chase was on again.

One evening, at a point between the Illinois and Wauhillau rivers in what is now Cherokee County, the outlaws were overtaken by the pursuers. A brief gunfight ensued with two of the robbers being killed. The remaining four jumped back onto their horses, grabbed the reins to the pack mules, and forded the Illinois River, about two miles from Chimney Rock. From this point they fled toward the forested hills in the distance.

The heavily laden mules were slowing the harried outlaws and the men decided it would be best to take cover and defend themselves against the persistent pursuers. As they rode toward Chimney Rock, now looming in the distance, a third outlaw was shot out of his saddle. Without pausing to ascertain whether or not the man was dead, the others spurred their mounts toward the safety of the woods, finally entering a thick stand of trees near the base of Chimney Rock. Here they dismounted and sought cover from which to defend themselves against the Louisianans.

The ensuing gunfight lasted well into the night with no casualties to either side. Fearing they would be overtaken if they fled with the heavily laden and now very tired mules, the outlaws, using the cover of darkness, decided to hide the gold in the many rock crevices they found near the base of Chimney Rock. Dividing the loot into several small portions, they wedged the gold into nearby crevices which they then covered over with dirt and forest debris.

Running low on ammunition, the outlaws decided to make a break from their position and ride deeper into Indian Territory where they believed they would be safe from further pursuit. They intended to return at a later date to retrieve the gold they had hidden in the cracks of the weathered limestone rock.

Just before dawn broke over an adjacent ridge, the remaining three outlaws dashed from the woods on horseback. The pursuers, anticipating such a maneuver, intercepted them between Tahlequah and Fourteen Mile Creek. All three outlaws were killed during the subsequent gun battle.

The Louisianans were convinced the gold was cached somewhere in the woods near the base of Chimney Rock where the outlaws hid during the night. The bandits were observed carrying the gold into the woods but they obviously did not have it in their possession when they fled from their hiding place. Returning to the site, the Louisianans searched a wide area for the rest of the day, but were unable to locate any of the gold. Dejected, they returned home.

Many who have searched for the gold near the base of Chimney Rock believe that the outlaws disguised the hiding places to look exactly like the surrounding forest. As the search continues, Chimney Rock, like a lone sentinel, stands above the surrounding forest, mutely guarding the fortune in gold hidden near its base.

The Innkeeper's Bad Luck

The old Indian had traveled many days on foot before arriving at the inn just outside the Tahlequah settlement. He stood at the bottom of the wooden steps leading up to the wide front doors and kicked the road dust from his moccasins. Adjusting the pack on his back, the Indian climbed the steps and entered the inn.

The innkeeper looked warily upon the old man as he came through the door. He had seen this type before—travelers with no money who would occasionally check into the inn, stay for a few days, and disappear in the middle of the night without paying the bill. The year was 1895, a recent drought made times hard, and few travelers carried much money.

The Indian approached the desk and inquired about a room. Eyeing the traveler suspiciously, the innkeeper noted the ragged and filthy clothes. He was about to have the Indian ejected from the premises when the traveler pulled out a roll of currency and asked the price of a room for a week. Seeing the large wad of money changed the innkeeper's attitude, and he forthwith assigned a room to the old man, collecting for a week in advance.

During the next few days, the innkeeper observed that the visitor would rise early in the morning and leave without eating breakfast. Somewhere he had obtained a horse and would ride out into the Ozark hills east of town. The Indian would stay gone all day, returning after sundown and immediately retiring to his room. The innkeeper was curious about the business of the

Indian and was inclined to inquire, but the old man always managed to avoid any conversation.

At the end of the week, the Indian approached the innkeeper and asked for an audience with him. Taking the Indian into his office, the innkeeper motioned him to a chair and poured him some coffee. The Indian came immediately to the point of his visit and related to the innkeeper a remarkable story of a buried fortune in gold somewhere in the hills to the east.

The Indian explained that he was a member of the Cherokee tribe and recited a long and impressive lineage that suggested he was related to chieftains and important elders of the tribe. Growing impatient with the old man's genealogy, the innkeeper encouraged him to get on with the story.

The Cherokee unfolded a tale about Chief Blackface, so called because of his mixed Seminole and African ancestry. Blackface and his followers made their camp in the densely wooded Ozark hills of the Cherokee and Choctaw nations in northeastern Oklahoma during the early part of the 1830s. Never one to take to the sedentary life of farming and raising a family, Blackface and his cutthroats resorted to attacking, robbing, and often killing travelers, prospectors, traders, and even other Indians who chanced near their hiding place.

One day one of Blackface's scouts reported the approach of a large Mexican pack train winding its way through the rugged hills nearby, apparently bound for St. Louis. With no warning, the renegade Indians charged out of the hills and attacked the pack train. The battle was brief and by the time the dust had cleared, all of the Mexicans lay dead on the trail. The Indians rounded up one hundred mules, most of which were carrying packs filled with gold bars.

With his small Indian army, Blackface herded the mules into the hills toward a secluded cave. There he unloaded the gold from the animals and carried it deep into the cave.

Several weeks later, Blackface and his followers attempted a raid on another pack train, but this time the muleteers were well-prepared. No sooner had the Indians charged out from hiding than the Mexicans circled their animals and began to fire away at the raiders. The battle raged for several hours, but Blackface's small and ill-armed force was no match for the Mexicans. Most of the Indians, including Blackface, were killed.

The old Cherokee told the innkeeper that as a child, he often heard this story from his grandfather who also professed to have knowledge of the location of the secret cave in the Ozarks that contained Blackface's cache of gold. The Cherokee told the innkeeper that he believed he was close to locating the cave but he was running low on money. If the innkeeper would allow him to remain at the inn for a few more days, he said, he would share the wealth with him when it was discovered.

The innkeeper was intrigued by the tale. Although suspicious, he agreed to allow the Indian to remain as a guest at the inn for a month while he searched for the treasure.

One evening, about two weeks later, the Indian rushed into the inn and gestured to the innkeeper that he needed to speak with him. Expecting an excuse, the innkeeper reluctantly waved the old man back into the office. There, visibly excited, the Indian related how he had finally located the lost cave of gold.

The innkeeper, excited by the Indian's discovery, suggested they leave immediately and retrieve the riches. The old man held up a hand and told the innkeeper that this must be done according to the Indian way. The Cherokee insisted the innkeeper be blindfolded on the journey to the cave and would be allowed to remove the cover only when in sight of the treasure. The innkeeper argued, but the Indian was adamant. Finally he agreed to be blindfolded.

The next morning the two rode to the edge of the clearing in which the inn was located and into the woods. Once they were out of sight, the Cherokee covered the innkeeper's head with a sack made of a dark coarse material. The sack was secured around his neck, making it impossible for him to see. For several hours the Indian led the innkeeper on horseback along a twisting route. Finally they halted, dismounted, and walked to a rock ledge. At that point, the innkeeper, still blindfolded, heard the Indian moving some heavy rocks, presumably ones that were blocking the entrance to the cave. The Indian then told the innkeeper they would have to crawl some distance into the cave. The two men crawled on their hands and knees for nearly a half-hour before they were able to stop and rise to their full height. By this time the innkeeper's pants were torn and his knees were bleeding.

Once inside the large chamber, the Cherokee removed the blindfold and held his torch high to illuminate the cavern. When his eyes adjusted to the light, the innkeeper gasped as he looked upon the great fortune of which the Indian spoke. Against the far wall of the chamber stood six large containers that reminded him of huge butter churns. They were filled to the top with bars of gold, each one about twelve inches long. The innkeeper inspected one of the bars, scratching into it with a knife, and determined that it was fashioned from the purest gold he had ever seen.

Overtaken with excitement at witnessing this vast wealth, the innkeeper told the Cherokee he wanted to take the gold to the inn immediately. The Indian said that was not possible until certain Cherokee rituals were completed. The innkeeper objected, but the Indian was persistent and the innkeeper finally agreed to wait. The Indian said they would be able to remove the gold within one week.

Once again the innkeeper was blindfolded and led from the cave. They stopped at the entrance where he heard the Indian replace several stones. The two men then retraced the trail back to the inn, and when they reached the clearing the blindfold was removed. As it was late and he was weary, the innkeeper went immediately to bed.

The next morning the innkeeper went to check on the Cherokee only to discover he had apparently not spent the night in his room. Making inquiries, he learned that the Indian had gone into town the night before, had gotten into a fight, and stabbed a man to death. The police were summoned and the Cherokee took flight into the woods east of town with the law officers in pursuit.

The next evening the police returned, having been unable to capture the fleeing killer.

For many years following the experience, the innkeeper recalled to others his vision of the immense wealth that lay within a secret cave in the Ozarks. His dreams were filled with images of the large containers filled to the top with bars of gold. He cursed himself often for listening to the old Cherokee.

As time passed, the story of Chief Blackface's lost cache of gold became part of the legend and lore of the Seminole-Negroes who inhabit this part of the Indian Territory. Several members of the tribe searched for the lost treasure but apparently with no success. In 1905, an Oklahoma newspaper reported that several members of the tribe had finally located the lost cache, but it was later determined to be a hoax.

During the early 1930s, reports surfaced that the old Cherokee had been seen in the area. As recently as 1936, several Tahlequah residents were organizing to try to find the Indian, who by that time would have been quite old. They were never successful.

Locust Grove Gold

Somewhere in Ottawa County a few miles west of Miami,
Oklahoma, stands an old grove of locust trees. The grove is
adjacent to the low hills that mark the westernmost limit of the
Oklahoma Ozarks. Beneath the stand of locust trees may rest a
fortune in gold that has lain there undisturbed for nearly 150
years.

In April 1842, according to legend, a small band of Mexicans
was leading a pack train from Texas to St. Louis, skirting the
western fringes of the Ozark Mountains and trying to avoid the
unfamiliar terrain of deep and narrow canyons within the range.
They were miners transporting three mule-loads of gold, the
fruits of several years of hard labor in a long-forgotten gold mine
in Texas.

One of the members of the party observed a group of riders
approaching along the trail from the south at a rapid pace.
Fearing bandits, the Mexicans decided to hide their gold before
the group arrived, intending to return for it when it seemed safe.

On the other side of a low rise, out of sight of the pursuers and
just off the trail, the Mexicans hastily dug a shallow trench. From
the mules they unloaded the deerskin sacks heavy with gold and
deposited them in the excavation.

After covering the hole, one of the Mexicans pulled from his
pocket a small leather sack of locust seeds and sprinkled several
handfuls atop the freshly turned earth. He explained to his
comrades that, should they find it necessary to vacate the area
for an extended period of time before returning for the gold, the
locust seedlings that would soon sprout would serve as a marker

for the buried fortune in gold.

The Mexicans mounted their horses and continued to ride northeastward, hoping to give their pursuers the impression that they were merely a group of poor men on a journey and not worth the trouble to rob.

The riders eventually caught up with the Mexicans several miles farther along the trail and killed all but one. The survivor was picked up two days later by a migrating band of Peoria Indians. The Peorias cared for the wounded Mexican for several weeks, but his wounds were serious and it was apparent he would not live much longer. Just before he died, he called the chief of the tribe to his side and told him of the three mule-loads of gold he and his companions buried along the trail near the Ozark hills. He expressed gratitude to the chief for trying to save him and explained he wished for him to have the gold for his tribe. He provided directions to the site and told about planting the locust seeds.

The Peoria Indians were not a people concerned with great wealth, and the story of the buried gold meant little to them.

Twenty years later, the Peorias were relocated to Ottawa County, where they settled into a routine of farming and raising horses on the good land near the low rolling hills of the Ozarks. Baptiste Peoria, chief of the tribe, recalled the tale of the dying Mexican and noted that the new home of the Peorias was near the area he described. In 1868, Baptiste Peoria discovered a locust grove just off the main road leading to Missouri and declared it to be the one described by the Mexican.

The Peoria Indians no longer exist as a tribe, but those who claim to know say that the locust grove is still there. After nearly 150 years, the stand of trees has grown full and thick, covering nearly a quarter of an acre. There are many living in Ottawa County who still believe that the three mule-loads of gold hidden by the Mexican miners still lie just beneath the tree-shaded ground.

References

Allsopp, Fred W. *Folklore of Romantic Arkansas*, vol. 1. The Grolier Society, 1931.

Anderson, LaVere Schoenfelt. "When There Was Gold In Them Thar Hills." *Tulsa Daily World*, Mar. 22, 1931.

_____. "Buried Treasure in the Devil's Promenade." *Tulsa Daily World*, June 14, 1931.

_____. "Death Haunts the Trail of Buried Slave Gold." *Tulsa Daily World*, June 21, 1931.

Bowers, Rodney. "Looking for Lost Spanish Mine." *Arkansas Gazette*, Sept. 25, 1988.

"Buried Treasures Were Never Found." *Wilburton (Oklahoma) News*, Nov. 24, 1905.

Collins, Earl A. *Legends and Lore of Missouri*. San Antonio, Texas: The Naylor Company, 1951.

Curlee, Mabel. "Hidden Treasure." *Baxter County History* 3.3, 1977.

Garland, Russell L. *Immigrants in the Ozarks*. Columbia: University of Missouri Press, 1939.

Hutchinson, H.B. "Daddy of Lead-Zinc Mines Tells His Story." *Daily Oklahoman*, May 11, 1930.

Jameson, W.C. "Tobe Inmon's Lost Silver Bullets." *True West* 33.3

(March 1986): 60-61.

_____. *Buried Treasures of the American Southwest.* Little Rock, Arkansas: August House, 1989.

Lambrecht, Gordon. "Gold." *Baxter County History* 1.4 (1975).

Leet, L. Don, and Judson, Sheldon. *Physical Geology.* Englewood Cliffs, New Jersey: Prentice-Hall, Inc., 1965.

McCall, Edith. "Lost Mines Discounted by Historian." *Branson Beacon,* December 16, 1982.

McCulloch, James A. "Another Piece in the Yoachum Puzzle." *Treasure Search* 16.6 (Nov.-Dec. 1988): 6-10, 26.

Morrow, Lynn, and Saults, Dan. "The Yoachum Silver Dollar: Sorting Out the Strands of an Ozarks Frontier Legend." *Gateway Heritage* (Winter, 1984-85): 8-15.

Pipes, Gerald H. *Lost Treasures of Table Rock Lake.* Reeds Spring, Missouri: Ozark Books, 1959.

Rafferty, Milton D. *The Ozarks: Land and Life.* Norman: University of Oklahoma Press, 1980.

Rascoe, Jesse. *Oklahoma Treasures Lost and Found.* Fort Davis, Texas: Frontier Book Company, 1974.

Ross, S.W. "Tales of Hidden Treasure along the Illinois." *Tulsa Daily World,* June 28, 1931.

_____. "Old Nation Indians Seek Lucky Cherokee." *Tulsa Daily World,* February 23, 1936.

Steele, Phillip. *Lost Treasures of the Ozarks.* Springdale, Arkansas: published by author.

Tatham, Robert L. *Missouri Treasures and Civil War Sites.* Boulder, Colorado: H. Glenn Carson Enterprises, 1974.

_____. *Ozark Treasure Tales.* Ragtown, Missouri: R.L. Tatham Co., 1979.

Wilson, Steve. *Oklahoma Treasure and Treasure Tales.* Norman: University of Oklahoma Press, 1984.

W. C. JAMESON, an environmentalist, folklorist, geographer, and musician, grew up in west Texas, studied in Oklahoma, and lives in Arkansas. The author of *Buried Treasures of the American Southwest* and numerous articles, he is currently the editor of *Mid-South Geographer* and a professor of geography at the University of Central Arkansas.

Other Books and Audiobooks from August House

Civil War Ghosts
Edited by Martin H. Greenberg, Charles G. Waugh,
and Frank D. McSherry, Jr.
Paperback / ISBN 0-87483-173-3

Confederate Battle Stories
Edited by Martin H. Greenberg, Charles G. Waugh,
and Frank D. McSherry, Jr.
Paperback / ISBN 0-87483-191-1

Ghost Stories from the American South
Compiled and edited by W. K. McNeil
Paperback / ISBN 0-935305-84-3

Tales of An October Moon
Four frightening, original stories from New England
Created and performed by Marc Joel Levitt
Audiobook / ISBN 0-87483-209-8

Buried Treasures of the Civil War
W. C. Jameson
Audiobook / ISBN 0-87483-492-9

Half Horse, Half Alligator
A Publishers Weekly Best Audio of the Year
Performed by Bill Mooney
Audiobook / ISBN 0-87483-494-5

A Field Guide to Southern Speech
Charles Nicholson
Paperback / ISBN 0-87483-098-2

August House Publishers P.O. Box 3223 Little Rock, AR 72203
800-284-8784